The Magical Stone Cottage

The Magical Stone Cottage

Shirley Cochran

To order additional copies of this book, contact:
Xlibris Corporation
1-888-795-4274
www.Xlibris.com
Orders@Xlibris.com
36022

Chapter 1

The young woman was engrossed in her thoughts as she walked along the narrow street on the outskirts of the village where she had lived all her life. The past week had been very unsettling and her heart felt bruised and battered. Her mother was in the final days of her life as she battled the disease that was stripping her of the beauty and dignity that had always been a part of her. As Anna walked along the dusty, narrow street, losing the one person who meant the most to her was a searing, ripping pain that threatened to tear her heart from her body. This was the first time that she had left her mother's side in a week, as she had even slept on a pallet on the hard, cold floor in order to be near in case she was needed. Today, her mother's sister had come for a visit and asked Anna for some time with her sister so that they could speak of private things. Anna had nowhere in particular to go, but it was a beautiful sunny day with just a hint of chill in the air, so she just began walking aimlessly and thinking about the life she had shared with her mother.

Anna was an only child, and her father had died when she was too young to really remember much about him. All she had were vague recollections of feeling safe when he held her in his arms and the smell of animals, tobacco and outdoors on his coat that she loved to snuggle her face into. As the young woman thought back over the years, she realized how difficult it must have been for her mother to provide for the two of them, but she had made it seem easy because she had always been happy and loving when they were together. The thought of never seeing that smile again caused a physical pain in her chest, and she wanted to cry out against the injustice.

Tears streamed down her cheeks in a torrent but they did nothing to ease the unbearable agony in her heart.

She had no idea how long she had walked when she looked around and realized she didn't recognize anything. She had roamed the countryside since she was a young child and was familiar with everything for many miles around, but she had never seen this area before. Just ahead she saw a lovely stone cottage and decided to inquire within for help finding her way home. She paused at the gate and stood looking in wonder at the beautiful little house. It sat in a forest of flowers and trees that seemed to hold it in their embrace. As she walked up the cobbled path she caught glimpses of movement out of the corner of her eyes but when she turned to look, nothing was there. Everything felt strange and yet as she walked up the path a deep feeling of comfort seemed to seep into her and she felt a peace she had never experienced before. The flowers and trees were a riot of color more deep and vibrant than anything she had ever seen before, and they seemed to be alive in a way that she could never have imagined. It was as though they were communicating with her on some level, and as she stopped to look at one small, vibrant violet bloom, she thought for a moment it had looked up at her and smiled. She stepped back in surprise and chided herself for having such fanciful thoughts.

The path to the door seemed much longer than she had thought, and when she looked back she could no longer see the road. She finally reached the door and knocked lightly. The door opened to reveal a very small, strange looking little man with a large, bulbous nose smiling at her as though they were old friends. He beckoned to her to enter, and she stepped through the door onto the smooth stone floor to find herself in a small room that somehow felt familiar and welcoming. Light streamed through large open windows and danced on the floor making patterns that appeared to be alive, and the air was filled with the heady scent of many flowers. She turned to ask the little man for directions only to find that he had disappeared, which was very strange, as there didn't appear to be any way out of the room except through the door that she was standing in. This should have been frightening, but instead of fear she felt a peace and joy that was totally unreasonable under the circumstances. She glanced around and felt as though she was trespassing with no right to be here, but she just could not bring herself to turn and walk out.

As she continued to look around, she noticed a table in the center of the room that she was sure had not been there when she first entered. It seemed as if the room and its furnishings changed each time she looked. This struck her as very odd, but still she felt no fear. There was a book on the table, and she walked over to take a look at it thinking that perhaps it would explain things. As she looked down at the cover of the book, her breath caught in her throat for the title of the book was "Anna's Life." She reached tentatively and opened it to the first page. There was no introduction, table of contents or any of the things normally found in books. The story began on the first page with the birth of a baby girl to very proud, loving parents.

There was one chair at the table and Anna sat down and began to read the book. As she read, she was suddenly able to recall memories of events that happened even when she was an infant. She realized that she had been a very lucky girl because of the depth of love she had known from her first moment of life. She felt again the comfort and safety that she had always felt in the arms of her father and mother. As the story continued and she grew older, there were memories of hurts and disappointments as well as the happy memories. The greatest of the hurtful memories was the loss of her father. Perhaps because she had been too young to understand what death was, she had felt the loss more deeply than anyone could have imagined. She felt again the confusion and remembered wondering if he had left because she had been bad and he no longer loved her as hot, salty tears rolled down her cheeks.

She continued to read and at times smile or weep as the memories came flooding back. Finally she came to the day that her mother's sister came to visit her very ill mother, and her hand trembled as she reached to turn the page. She hesitated for a moment and then turned the page only to find that the rest of the book was blank. Anna sat in stunned silence not knowing whether she was relieved or angry. Everything in the cottage had seemed so perfect, and she realized that she had expected to learn that her mother was going to get well and everything would be wonderful the way it had always been before. It seemed that the book had served no real purpose at all. There were many pages left in the book, but they were all blank, and she felt betrayed.

As Anna sat lost in thought, she heard a small voice telling her that the book had been placed there to help her recall memories to bring her comfort. The voice explained that the rest of the pages had not yet been written because it was up to her to make what she would of the rest of her life. Anna looked around to see where the voice had come from, but there was no one else in the cottage. This was, indeed, a very strange place, and she was surprised once again that she felt no fear. She marveled at the fact that she could accept all that was happening with wonder and joy rather than fear. She sat for a long time thinking back over her life and wishing that she had been more helpful to her mother.

Suddenly, Anna glanced up as she sensed movement across the room and saw the figure of a man standing in the shaft of sunlight that poured into the room through one of the windows. Though she could not see his features clearly, he seemed very familiar and suddenly she knew that he was her father. He began to speak to her about life and what it is really all about. He told her that he had never left her but only stepped through a thin veil that separates the physical world from the world of spirit and that he had always been there watching over her and her mother. He explained that the time had come for her mother to join him on the other side of the veil, but he wanted her to know that they would both be with her always. He explained that life was not just a single event but rather a continuous journey of birth, death and rebirth until each soul managed to make its way back to the source through growth and learning. She sat in silence as he talked and felt a stirring deep within her being and a feeling of something opening. Finally, he told her it was time for her to go back the way she had come and return to her mother's side.

She rose from the chair and took one last look around. As she walked to the door, she saw several small figures moving around the room and some flying through the air. She was amazed that she had not been able to see them before and realized that she was seeing on a different level than she had ever seen before. She stepped through the door and saw that there were many more small figures working tending the plants. She moved along the path reluctant to have this magical time come to an end. Suddenly she found herself back on a familiar road and looked around in confusion. There was no sign of the cottage, and she turned to hurry home. So much had happened that it seemed she must have been gone for a long time, but as she entered the house and looked at the clock she realized that she had only been gone for about 30 minutes.

Anna's aunt called out to her from the room where her mother lay and she hurried to her mother's side. There was a look of peace on her mother's face as she smiled up at Anna and Anna realized that somehow she knew what had happened. She felt a bond that was much deeper than any she had ever felt before and knew that the time had come to say goodbye and let her mother move away from the pain and suffering she was experiencing. She bent and kissed the beloved forehead and whispered, "I love you, go in peace." With one last smile, Anna's mother let out a long breath and slipped gently away. As the breath ended, the figure she had seen earlier in the cottage appeared in the corner of the room and was joined by the figure of her mother that rose from the now empty body lying on the bed.

Anna turned to comfort her aunt with a heart at once heavy with grieve and at the same time a joy beyond anything she had ever known. She was unable to explain to anyone why in the weeks and years that followed she never grieved the way that most people did over the death of those they loved.

Chapter 2

Anna awoke to the sound of birds singing and the sun pouring through the window onto her bed. She sat up and saw that it was a beautiful spring day and then felt a lump come into her throat as she remembered this was to be the day of her mother's funeral and her last day in the only home she had known her entire life. Anna and her Aunt Helen had talked in the three days since her mother's passing about Anna's plans for the future. Her mother had worked hard just to provide essentials and there had never been anything to put aside. However, after Anna had finished school the previous summer and began working at whatever jobs she could get locally, her mother had insisted she save whatever she made, so she had managed to save a small amount. Anna realized now that her mother had known she would need this money very soon and once again felt gratitude for the very special woman who had been her mother. She had already tried to find work here and knew that there were no jobs in this small village. She knew she would have to go somewhere else, but she had never lived anywhere else, and the idea of leaving this safe haven and going to a strange town was very frightening. She was very relieved when Aunt Helen suggested she come stay with her until she could get established in a job and find a place of her own. She had visited Aunt Helen once when she was very small, but she had missed her mother so badly that she would never go again. The only thing she could remember about the town where her aunt lived was that it had seemed very big and noisy and people were always in a hurry and never smiled at each other. Anna knew that she would have to find something for herself soon because the house where her aunt lived was very small and three of her cousins were still living there.

Anna and Helen had gone through the few possessions she and her mother had and packed those things she was to take with her. As she looked at the small pile of belongings, Anna wondered how so little could be left from an entire lifetime, but she heard a small voice whisper that what her mother had given her were things of the heart and not worldly possessions. It still surprised Anna when this voice whispered to her, but she was becoming more accustomed to it, and it seemed somehow comforting. She no longer looked for the source as she had before because she knew that there was nothing to be seen.

Anna had made a point of going away from others out into nature for a while each day since she had come upon the stone cottage in hopes of seeing her mother and father. Though she had not seen them, she still retained the ability to see the nature spirits, and when she was among them she felt the peace and joy that she had felt in the cottage. She was even beginning to be able to see some of the spirits in town, especially in the home she had shared with her mother, but it seemed they were not as happy there. She wondered how she was going to manage to keep in touch with this when she got to the town where her aunt lived with all of the noise and bustle. However, whenever she thought about this, she heard the small voice telling her not to worry because everything was as it should be.

The day after the funeral Anna gathered her meager belongings and gave the key to the little house where she had been so happy to the lady next door. She and Aunt Helen walked to the train station and boarded the train that would take her to her new life. Anna was young, and with the resilience of youth she began to feel a hint of excitement mixed with the apprehension of leaving everything that was familiar and stepping into the unknown. Aunt Helen fell asleep shortly after telling Anna she should get some rest, but Anna's emotions were much too unsettled for her to be able to sleep. As the countryside changed from the familiar to the unfamiliar, Anna began to feel lonely for the first time and realized how truly blessed she had been having lived around people she had known all her life.

The train sped across the landscape all day, and it was after dark before they arrived at the station in the town where Aunt Helen lived. Anna had fallen asleep for short periods of time, but she was tired and very glad to leave the train and be able to move around. As they stepped off the train, a man approached and kissed Aunt Helen on the cheek and gave Anna a hug. This was obviously her Uncle Ted, and Anna was relieved to be welcomed so warmly. She did not remember Uncle Ted from her visit many years ago and had wondered if he would resent having her come stay with them. Aunt Helen and Uncle Ted talked about the everyday things that had occurred while she had been gone and Anna found this somehow comforting. They talked about how he had coped with the children in her absence and had a few laughs at his descriptions of the mishaps he had encountered in trying to do those things that Aunt Helen made look so simple. It was obvious that they were very glad to be together again, and Anna thought about how happy her own parents must be now that they were together.

When they arrived at Aunt Helen's and Uncle Ted's, her cousins all gathered around Aunt Helen to hug her and talk to her. They were all talking at once, and Anna had never heard such a den. She stood back and smiled at the obvious love and happiness of this family. After a few minutes everything had settled down, and Aunt Helen went to Anna's side and drew her into the center of the room where the others were. She introduced her to each of the cousins beginning with Stella who was 12, Ruth who was 14, and finally Joan who was 17. Since Stella and Ruth already shared a room, Anna would be sharing Joan's room.

They had a wonderful dinner that the girls and their father had prepared to celebrate their mother's return and then sat a long time at the table talking. By the time dinner was over and the kitchen cleaned up it was quite late. Anna was very tired and fell asleep quickly feeling safe among loving, caring people.

She awoke early the next morning with energetic enthusiasm eager to search for a job and begin her new life. She dressed and went downstairs where she found Aunt Helen already busy preparing breakfast for everyone. Anna's mother had taught her from an early age to help with household chores and she naturally began helping prepare the meal. The two women spoke softly while they worked side by side. A rapport had developed between them in the days after her mother's death as they handled all the details of the funeral and preparation for Anna's move. The peace and quiet was soon shattered as the others came downstairs and the day began. The girls were still in school, so they were soon gone and Uncle Ted had left for work. Aunt Helen had told her that she would take her later to check on some possible positions and show her around a little. The house settled once again into quiet as Anna and Aunt Helen went about cleaning and putting the house in order for the day.

The house needed a lot of work with Helen having been gone for most of a week, but she was surprised at how fast the work went with Anna helping. Unlike her daughters, Anna seemed to know what needed to be done without being told, and was a very good worker. By ten o'clock the house had been brought to order and Aunt Helen assisted Anna in dressing properly. Most of the clothes Anna had were only suitable for wear around the house, and they discussed the need to shop for some things that would be better suited for wear in town. Anna had told Aunt Helen about the money she had saved and fortunately there was enough to buy the essentials and still have enough left for whatever she would need until she found employment. Aunt Helen talked to Anna about how good she was at household chores and asked if she would mind working as a domestic. Though Anna had finished school and was a good student, she had no experience dealing with people on a large scale and they agreed this would serve as a good start.

They visited several of Helen's friends and got a few names of people to contact about employment. Aunt Helen used the excuse that Anna was unfamiliar with the city to accompany her as she made inquiries. She was, in fact, concerned because Anna was so trusting and had no experience with people who would take advantage of her. They made a few purchases and followed several leads that day without success, and it was soon time to return home to prepare the evening meal. Helen assured Anna that she would soon have a job and should not worry because they loved having her with them.

They were both tired as they began the meal but that was soon forgotten in the bustle as the rest of the family returned home. They each talked about their day over dinner and Anna listened with interest. The girls were all excited as they talked about their boyfriends. This was Anna's first exposure to girl talk on this level, and she listened as the girls talked about the intricacies of their relationships. Anna had only had one boyfriend, and their relationship had been nothing like what her cousins talked about. She and Wesley had been the only young people in the village who were close to the same age, so it was only natural that they become close friends. Wesley had kissed her gently on the lips several times, and they had even talked about someday getting married, but there had been none of the fire and excitement that her cousins exhibited when they discussed their boyfriends. It seemed that everything in her life was going to be very different now, and Anna wondered if she would ever fit in and be comfortable with this life.

For the next two days Anna and her aunt set out each day on their quest. The weekend came without them having found anything, and Aunt Helen told Anna they should just relax for a few days and try again on Monday. Anna's older cousin Jeff came over on Saturday with his laundry. He had a small apartment on the other side of town and seldom managed to get by during the week, but Aunt Helen told Anna he never missed coming on the weekend to get his laundry done. Aunt Helen had a washing machine, and Anna loved to do laundry using this. She and her mother had always done the laundry using a washboard and brush, and it seemed almost like a miracle to Anna that you could just put the clothes in and have a machine move them back and forth to get them clean. Although Aunt Helen and Uncle Ted's home was small, it seemed very luxurious to Anna and she enjoyed helping care for it.

Anna watched her four cousins in awe as they teased each other, but Jeff and the girls went out of their way to include Anna in their revelry. Everyone pitched in and helped prepare a large midday meal and laughed as they tripped over each other. Aunt Helen's kitchen had seemed large to Anna until they all tried to get in there at the same time. After they had eaten, and the kitchen was put to rights, they all went out into the backyard to relax. Jeff and the girls invited Anna to play games with them, but after a short while she asked to be excused because she was very tired. She lay on the grass under a tree and watched them play and thought about how different her life was now. It had only been one week since her mother's funeral, and yet it seemed like a much longer time because her days had been so full and there had been so many changes.

As she lay on the grass, she began to catch movements out of the corner of her eyes and soon was able to see the elementals as they went about their work in the small backyard. She fell asleep lying on the grass, and dreamt that her mother and father came to kiss her cheeks and tell her they loved her. She only slept for a short while, as the sun was getting low in the sky, and it was becoming cooler. Everyone went into the house and sat around the kitchen table eating leftovers while the cousins argued about who had really won at the games they had played. Jeff stayed over and slept on the sofa in order to go to church the next morning with the family, and they all went to bed tired and happy.

Sunday morning was chaos with everyone getting ready for church with only one bathroom, and them laughing and teasing each other. Anna was surprised at the casual way all of the cousins ran around partially dressed from room to room asking to borrow things. She dressed hurriedly and went downstairs to wait and once again, she wondered if she would ever be able to fit in. As Jeff and the girls came downstairs they teased Anna about being so modest and joked about how red her face had been. At first she felt bad, but as they walked past they each gave her a hug, and she knew that they were not being mean but only trying to make her feel more comfortable.

They walked the short distance to church. The cousins were still in high spirits, and Aunt Helen reminded them several times that it was Sunday, and they should be less boisterous. Anna saw that her aunt had trouble keeping a stern face as she chastised her offspring, and her pride in them was obvious. As they entered the church, Anna looked around in wonder. She had never been in a building so large and beautiful. Light poured through the stained glass windows and made them seem to come to life. All of the wood was of a dark, rich mahogany and shone as though with a light of its own. The music from the organ seemed to penetrate into her body and Anna's heart soared with the beauty of it all. Uncle Ted led the way to a pew and they all filed in and sat down. Announcements were made about events that were coming up and then everyone sang three or four songs after which the pastor went to the pulpit and began his sermon. As he began to preach Anna felt as though she were being assaulted. He paced back and forth, yelled and pointed his finger at the congregation and threatened them with hell. Anna had attended the small church in her village all her life and the message had always been of a loving God who cared about his people and encouraged them to live a good life and love and help each other. This was Anna's first experience of a vengeful God who demanded absolute obedience or threatened an eternity of suffering. Anna wondered how there could be so much beauty and so much ugliness in the same place, and as they left the church, she hoped that she would not have to ever come back.

Chapter 3

The following day Anna and Aunt Helen set out once again in search of employment for Anna. After several hours they had been unable to find any leads and stopped to get a cup of tea and think about possible ways to proceed. As they talked and sipped their tea, they overheard two well-dressed ladies at a nearby table talking about how difficult it was to find good help. The older of the two ladies was telling her friend that she had just fired her maid because she caught her stealing. Helen approached the ladies and apologized for interrupting. She told them that her niece was new to the city and was looking for employment as a domestic, and the lady invited Anna to come over and began questioning her about her qualifications. Anna explained that she had only finished school the year before and had never had a full-time job but had always helped with chores at home and worked at a variety of jobs doing whatever she could find since finishing school. They talked for quite some time and Anna's demeanor impressed the lady who told them that her name was Mrs. Burke and gave them a card with her address. They agreed that Anna would be given a room and be paid a minimal amount until she had proven herself at which time her salary would be increased. She would be off on Sundays unless she was needed to help with some special event, which Mrs. Burke assured her would seldom happen and that she would be allowed to take time off as compensation. They then arranged for Anna to arrive at Mrs. Burke's home the following afternoon, and Helen assured Mrs. Burke that she would help Anna get there since she did not know her way around.

As they walked home both women were lost in thought. Anna was not sure whether she was happy or sad. She felt safe with her aunt's family and was uncertain about her ability to survive on her own where everything was so different from what she was accustomed to. She was beginning to worry when she heard the small voice whisper that everything was as it should be and would work out for her good. Helen had her own fears for Anna; however, Mrs. Burke had seemed like a kind woman, and Anna would be able to visit, so she would still be able to advise and watch over her to some extent.

That night at the dinner table Anna joined the conversation talking enthusiastically about her job and going to live with Mrs. Burke. Uncle Ted remarked how fortunate she had been to find a position so soon, but Anna knew that it was not just good fortune that was responsible. She and Joan talked late into the night about the things that all young girls talk about. Anna had read books about romance but had never imagined experiencing it. Now that she was here where so much was happening all around her, she began to think about what it would be like to experience romantic love and felt a rush of enthusiasm for her new life. She fell asleep with a sense of her mother and father close and comforting.

The following morning Anna said goodbye to her cousins and Uncle Ted. She and Aunt Helen shopped for a few things for her and then packed her things and set out for the Burke's home. Aunt Helen knew that it was quite a long way on the other side of the city, so she inquired as to which bus would take them closest and where they should get off. They had to change buses once and Aunt Helen made a note of which buses they were taking and the stops so Anna could catch the bus to come visit whenever she was able to get away. As they rode through the city, Anna gazed in wonder at the sights of the stores and all the people hurrying through the streets. They all seemed to know where they were going and be in a great hurry to get there, and never once did she see anyone smile or stop to exchange a word with someone else. Anna could not help thinking how lonely they all looked and began to long for the people of her small village who had been so friendly and caring.

They soon moved out of the center of the city and into the outskirts where homes were spaced wider apart with areas of natural landscape. Anna began to feel more at home and looked around her with interest. The countryside here was less rocky and rugged than where she had lived, and she found the softly rolling hills with their open fields very beautiful and inviting.

Aunt Helen had told the bus driver the address they needed and asked him to let them know when the reached the stop closest to that address. After about 30 minutes the driver told them that this was the closest he could take them and they got out at the street on the card Mrs. Burke had given them. It was a beautiful spring day and Anna's spirits began to lift at being in the open countryside. As they walked, Aunt Helen talked to Anna about how she should approach the Burkes and things she should avoid doing. She was not concerned because Anna was such a quiet, polite girl but merely wanted to make it as easy as possible for Anna. They passed two very large houses, but the addresses did not match that on the card. After walking for perhaps 20 minutes, they rounded a curve in the road and saw another house before them. It was a lovely two-storied house built of natural stone and wood set among gardens that were in full spring bloom. It was very beautiful and Anna hoped this was where she would be living. The house was smaller than the other houses they had passed, but it had a charm that she found very inviting. As they approached the gate Anna strained to read the number and then smiled as she saw that it was indeed the address Mrs. Burke had given them.

They followed the gravel drive around to the back of the house and walked toward a door with the top half open. As they approached, a plump, middle-aged woman with ruddy cheeks looked up and smiled. The woman came over and introduced herself as Mrs. Connors, the housekeeper. Aunt Helen explained that Anna was the new maid and she had accompanied her because she was new to the area and didn't know her way around. Mrs. Connors invited them both in and offered them a cup of tea. There was a long table in the middle of the kitchen and Mrs. Connors motioned for them to sit while they drank their tea and rested from their long walk. She told Anna that her duties would be to assist her with the cooking and cleaning and explained in some detail what this would entail. After they had finished their tea and rested a bit, Mrs. Connors took them to a neat room off the kitchen that be would Anna's. The room was small with one window that faced east and Anna was very happy that she would wake to the morning sun shining on the bed. She placed her small suitcase on the comfortable looking bed and assured Mrs. Connors that the room was very wonderful. Mrs. Connors told Anna she would show her the rest of the house after she had unpacked and then she could take the rest of the day to get settled and acquaint herself with the house and grounds.

Back in the kitchen Anna had just turned to say goodbye to her aunt when Mrs. Burke entered the room. She welcomed Anna and Helen to her home and inquired about their trip from the city. On learning that they had walked from the bus stop, she told Mrs. Connors to summon her husband, who also worked for the Burkes, to drive Helen back to the bus stop. The two women said goodbye to Helen and Anna followed her outside to say goodbye. Helen felt very relieved after meeting Mrs. Connors and seeing how warmly Mrs. Burke had welcomed Anna. She gave Anna a hug and told her that she should come visit whenever she could. Anna thanked her aunt for all that she had done to help her and kissed her on the cheek as tears filled her eyes.

After unpacking her things and putting them away, Anna returned to the kitchen to see if she was needed to help with anything. Mrs. Connors took her on a tour of the house pointing out where linens and cleaning supplies were kept and then began to prepare dinner. Anna helped by preparing the vegetables that were on the table and marveled at the kitchen, which was as large as the entire cottage where Anna and her mother had lived. There was a large stove with two ovens below and warming ovens above. There were baskets of fruits and vegetables in a room below the kitchen and a large pantry filled with jars of preserved fruits and vegetables. The door that led outside could be opened all the way or just the top half. There were two windows across the room from the stove with large ledges on which two pies were cooling. The air was full of wonderful smells and Anna's mouth began to water as she realized she had not eaten since breakfast. Mrs. Connors saw her looking at the pies and asked if she was hungry. Anna answered in the affirmative and blushed at having been so obvious, and Mrs. Connors cut her a large slice of a loaf of bread and smothered it with butter and jam. It was very delicious, and Anna longed to ask for another, but she knew that dinner would be ready soon. The sun was setting and Mrs. Connors closed the top part of the door and turned on several lamps as the kitchen became cool and dark. She then told Anna to follow her as she went through the house turning on lamps, closing windows and lighting fires that had previously been laid.

Anna watched as Mrs. Connors served dinner to Mr. and Mrs. Burke. Mrs. Connors had told Anna that the Burkes had a son, but he was away at college, so most of the time it was only the two of them unless they invited friends for dinner. Mr. Connors had entered the kitchen earlier and fixed himself a plate and sat down to eat. Once the family was served, Anna and Mrs. Connors joined Mr. Connors at the table in the kitchen to eat their own dinner. Anna was certain that Mrs. Connors was the best cook in the entire world. She had never seen such an array of delicious food prepared in such an appetizing way. Meals had been very simple for her and her mother and even at her aunt and uncle's home. She never dreamed there was food like this, and she was certain that she was going to like working here very much. While they ate, Mrs. Connors made trips to the dining room to clear dishes and serve additional courses in response to Mrs. Burke's bell. When Mr. and Mrs. Burke had finished eating, the table had been cleared and the dining room cleaned of any crumbs, Anna sat at the table and talked to Mr. and Mrs. Connors while they all finished their meal. They ate leisurely while getting to know each other, and when they had eaten and the kitchen was put to rights, Mrs. Connors told Anna she was free to do whatever she wished until the next morning when she would wake her to help with breakfast.

Anna decided to take a walk and work off some of the food she had eaten. She could not remember ever having eaten so much, but everything had been so good she just couldn't stop. She could understand why Mrs. Connors was so plump and knew that she would have to watch herself in the future to avoid becoming the same. The sun had set, but the moon was full and it was quite bright as Anna walked toward a small stream she saw behind the house. Being in the country with the sounds of the night brought mixed feelings of sadness and comfort because it seemed so much like home. Anna was happy here and knew that she had been brought to this place by something much larger than chance, but she could not help missing her mother.

She sat down on the cool, damp grass beside the stream and let herself become lost in the sounds of the water bubbling happily over the pebbles as it went on its way. After she had been there for a while, she became aware of movements and turning saw that there was a small village of tiny people living within a circle of trees to her left. She watched as they danced and listened closely to hear them singing. She watched as small fairies flew around her, and when she help out her hand one of them came and sat on her thumb. They were so delicate and beautiful, and she felt an expansion within herself. Anna knew this world had always been around and wondered why she had never been able to see it before and could now. Then she remembered the feeling of something opening inside her that she had experienced in the stone cottage the day her mother had died and realized this had something to do with it. As she turned to look around, she saw her mother and father arm in arm smiling at her, and her heart leapt with joy at how happy they looked.

Suddenly, there was a noise from the vicinity of the house that brought Anna sitting upright. When she looked around her she could no longer see any of the tiny people or her mother and father. She smiled as she thought how she had let her mind play tricks on her, but then she noticed a few sparkles on her thumb and knew that it had not been her imagination after all.

Chapter 4

Anna awoke early the next morning and stretched luxuriating in the softness of the mattress and linens. She was already dressed when Mrs. Connors tapped softly on her door and hurried to the kitchen eager to begin the day. As they worked preparing breakfast, Anna was once again amazed at the variety and amount of food, and she realized that she was very hungry even though she had eaten so much last night. Mrs. Connors was delighted with how capable Anna was for someone so young and how quickly she learned. Breakfast was soon served to the Burke's, and Anna sat down with Mr. and Mrs. Connors to eat while they talked about her duties and what to expect. She was told that the Burkes quite often took trips and during those times she would have most of her days to do whatever she wished.

When Mrs. Burke rang the bell, Mrs. Connors sent Anna to answer the summons. As Anna entered the dining room and approached Mrs. Burke, she was very nervous but felt reassured when Mrs. Burke looked up and smiled. Mrs. Burke introduced Anna as the new maid to Mr. Burke who welcomed her and said he hoped she would be happy with them. Anna thanked him and turned back to Mrs. Burke who told her she could remove the plates and bring them more coffee. As she entered the kitchen, she knew that Mrs. Connors had been watching and sensed that she was pleased with her. When they had finished eating, Mrs. Connors gave her husband a list of things that were needed from town explaining that he drove Mr. Burke to his office each morning and then did the shopping, so if she needed anything he could get it for her. Anna told them that she would like to write to her aunt and asked if he could get her some paper, envelopes, pencils and stamps. Mr. Connors replied that he would be glad to get these for her, whereupon she went to her room and returned with the money to pay for the items.

Anna and Mrs. Connors cleaned the dining room, kitchen and then the rest of the downstairs, and Anna worked happily enjoying the feel of the carved wood as she polished the beautiful furniture and woodwork and marveled at how the light played on the wood and gave it depth and life. Mrs. Connors explained that they never worked upstairs until Mrs. Burkes came back downstairs after breakfast, so when the downstairs was cleaned, they went to the kitchen to have a cup a tea while they waited and were discussing the food that was to be prepared for the rest of the day when they heard Mrs. Burke come downstairs. After gathering the cleaning supplies they would need for the upstairs. They entered the hallway and had started up the stairs when Mrs. Burke asked them to come into the parlor where she told them that she would be going into town for lunch and would not be home until later. She told Anna if she needed anything, to be sure to let Mrs. Connors know and then asked Mrs. Connors to stay for a private word.

Anna went on upstairs and entered the bathroom. She had cleaned the tub, sink and toilet and gathered the used towels into a pile when Mrs. Connors entered the room. Mrs. Connors showed her where to put the soiled linens and where the clean linens were and told Anna that the bed linens were changed twice weekly on Monday and Friday unless they were instructed to change them sooner. As this was Wednesday they only had to make the bed and dust and sweep the room, which was soon done, and Anna returned to the bathroom to mop the floor and then cleaned the hallway and stairs.

Mr. Connors returned around noon and they all sat down to eat a light lunch of leftovers from the night before. He gave Anna the things she had requested and her change, and she put these in her room. After they had eaten lunch, Mrs. Connors and Anna gathered the soiled linens and other dirty clothes and took them to the laundry room where Anna was instructed in the use of the washing machine. Anna enjoyed the hum of the washing machine as it moved the clothes first one way, and then the other, and she had always loved the smell of clean, wet laundry. It was a bright, sunny, spring day, and she laughed aloud as the gentle breeze caught the sheets and made sails of them as she hung them on the line. The laundry was soon done, and she returned to the kitchen to find Mrs. Connors preparing vegetables for cooking that evening.

They talked about the other rooms of the house that were not used daily, and she was told that the bedroom across from the Burke's room was cleaned weekly on Thursday so that it would be ready in case the Burke's son Jason should come home for the weekend. The other two bedrooms were cleaned twice a month or when guests were expected, and the rooms downstairs were cleaned daily except for the large room that was only used for large parties. This room was cleaned monthly or whenever it was to be used. Mrs. Connors told Anna that Mrs. Burke always gave plenty of notice so there was time to get everything ready for special events and that extra help was hired for cooking and cleaning for parties.

By four o'clock dinner was started and the clean laundry had been folded and put away, so Mrs. Connors told Anna she could relax until time for the final preparation at six o'clock and she would call her when she was needed. Anna went to her room, got the writing supplies and took them to sit by the stream to write to her aunt and her family. She told them about the house, how nice everyone was and how wonderful the food was. She thanked them for all they had done for her, especially for making her feel welcome and said she hoped to visit soon. When the letter was written and ready to be mailed, she lay back in the grass and watched the clouds overhead. She heard faint sounds and looked toward the circle of trees where once again she saw the little people going about their business.

After she had watched them for a while, she picked up the paper and pencil and began to draw the small village and the people who lived there. She had no training in art other than what she had gotten in school and her efforts were not very good. Her proportions were all wrong, and there was no depth to her drawings, but she continued sketching until she heard Mrs. Connors calling.

After dinner was over, and the evening chores were done, Anna went once again to sit beside the stream. She watched the little people and fairies for a while, but the evening had turned cold, and she soon returned to the house to warm by the fire in the kitchen.

On Saturday, Mrs. Connors asked what she was going to do on her day off tomorrow. Anna had not thought about it and had no idea what to do, and Mrs. Connors invited her to go to church with them. After the experience with her aunt's church she hesitated to do this, but she finally agreed, and the next morning she set off with the Connors for church. The service was more like those at home, so she enjoyed it very much and was glad she had come. They had cooked all of the food for that day on Saturday and after a light lunch Mr. and Mrs. Connors retired to their rooms to rest. Anna changed her clothes and decided to go for a walk across the countryside. She walked for a while and then sat down to rest on a large rock. The sun had warmed the rock, and she lay back to let the heat soak through her body. She closed her eyes and listened to the sounds all around her. It wasn't long before she heard the now familiar whispering sound of the little people, and when she looked she saw a lovely little village in the hollow of a large stump. All around the meadow the little people worked tending the flowers and trees. She had her paper and pencil with her, and she began to draw what she saw.

She heard a voice and looked up to find a young man standing beside the rock. She had been so engrossed in what she was doing that she had not heard his approach, and she blushed as she realized that he was looking down at her sketches. He smiled and apologized for snooping and backed away. The young man told her his name was Tom and that he lived in the house they could see in the distance. She immediately began to apologize for trespassing and was told not to worry because no one around here would get upset with her taking a walk across an unfenced meadow. She told him her name and that she was the maid for the Burkes. Tom sat beside her on the rock as they talked about the area. He told her about local dances and events that he thought she might enjoy and asked if she would like to attend a dance the following Saturday at the church she had attended that day. Anna was excited at the chance to meet others and told him she would love to go but did not know how to dance, and Tom replied that while he was certainly not an expert dancer he would be glad to teach her. She could tell from the sun that it was getting late, so she rose to leave, and he offered to walk with her part of the way to be certain she did not get lost.

As they walked, they talked about their childhoods, and she told him about the village where she had lived. When they came within sight of the Burke's house, Tom said goodbye and she agreed to meet him at the church the following Saturday evening. After dinner Anna went to sit by the stream and thought about the day. Watching the little people relaxed her and after about an hour she rose and walked back to the house. All around her she could see the little people moving among the plants and trees, and she saw there were many little groups of houses throughout the grounds. The fairies flew around her and landed on her shoulders and head, and she felt as though she were in a strange and wonderful world. That night Anna smiled in her sleep as she dreamed of being swept off her feet by a handsome knight.

The next week seemed to drag as she waited for Saturday to come. She told Mrs. Connors about meeting Tom and that he had invited her to the dance, and Mrs. Connors told her she knew Tom and that he was a nice boy from a good family. When Saturday came, Anna could hardly control her eagerness and began to fret as she noticed that the day was becoming threatening with dark clouds moving in. She voiced concern that she would be unable to get to the dance that evening, and because she seemed so disappointed Mr. Connors finally took pity on her. He told her that if it were raining, he would drive her and pick her up after the dance.

That evening Anna was very grateful that Aunt Helen had insisted she buy one dress that would be suitable for such an occasion. Mrs. Connors helped her fix her hair and told her she looked very pretty. Anna was not a beautiful girl, but the dress brought out the color of her eyes and with the heightened color in her cheeks and the sparkle in her eyes she did look quite pretty. It had rained that afternoon, but by the time Anna was ready to leave the late afternoon sun was shining brightly. The air was fresh and filled with the fragrance of flowers, as though the world had been washed clean, and she enjoyed the walk to the church.

When Anna arrived, Tom was waiting at the door to the church, and she was soon having so much fun she forgot about being nervous. He introduced her to everyone, and they treated her as though they had known her forever. Tom taught her some dance steps and soon had her twirling around the floor with confidence and between dances she got to know some of the others. A couple of the girls also worked for local families, and they told her the Burkes were known to be very good to work for.

When the dance was over, Tom walked her home, and she thanked him for inviting her and teaching her to dance. The sky was filled with stars, and they spoke in soft voices as they walked. He told her there would be another dance the next month and asked if she would like to go. She happily agreed, and since he lived on the other side of the church, they agreed to meet at the church as they had this time. The kitchen door was open when they arrived, and Mrs. Connors invited Tom in, but he declined as he had a long walk home. They said goodnight and Anna entered the kitchen where Mrs. Connors was having a cup of tea. Anna told her about the dance and the young people she had met as Mrs. Connors finished her tea.

Chapter 5

Anna settled into a comfortable routine of work and getting together with Tom and the others whenever she could. As the days grew longer, she sometimes met Tom when she went for long walks. She was treated very well and thought she was fortunate to be living in such luxury. She still found time to be alone and draw the little people and fairies, and her skill was improving day by day. She soon felt limited by the sketching and decided to try some color. They got paid at the end of the month, and she and Mrs. Connors accompanied Mr. Connors when he went to town to do some shopping. She was not paid much, but she still had some of the money she had saved when she was home with her mother, and since she had no real expenses, she felt quite wealthy. She purchased another dress and a few personal items, and then she asked Mrs. Connors where she could purchase some colored pencils and chalk for her drawing. They found a store that sold art supplies and Anna bought chalk, colored pencils and some special paper. On the way home Mrs. Connors asked about the art supplies and Anna explained she had been doing pencil drawings when she went to sit beside the stream. She made no mention of the fact that she really saw the things she drew. When they arrived at the house, she showed some of her better drawings to Mr. and Mrs. Connors and they complimented her on her ability.

Anna enjoyed her work and took pride in keeping the house spotlessly clean, and Mrs. Burke had told her how pleased she was with her. It had been about a month and a half since she started the job when Mrs. Burke announced that she and Mr. Burke were going to leave in a week and be gone for 10 days. She told Anna that she could take a few days off to visit her aunt and that Mr. Connors could drive her when he made a trip to town. Anna wrote a hasty letter that day and sent it with Mr. Connors to let her aunt know about the time off and received a reply a couple of days later telling her that they were looking forward to seeing her.

The Burkes left on the following Thursday and Anna worked to get everything done before she left for her visit. Mr. Connors drove her to her aunt's home Saturday morning and told her he would pick her up Wednesday morning. She had told her aunt when to expect her, and the entire family greeted her when she stepped out of the car. She introduced them to Mr. Connors who declined when Aunt Helen invited him in, because he said he needed to get back.

Everyone filed back into the house and gathered around the kitchen table where Aunt Helen had placed a large dish of cookies and a pitcher of fresh milk. Anna told them about her job and described the house, and they all said how happy they were for her. They then started teasing her about her boyfriend because she had written Aunt Helen about meeting Tom and going to the dance. The girls told her about their boyfriends and that Jeff even had a girlfriend now. After lunch Anna went shopping with Aunt Helen and the girls and bought another dress that they found on sale. The girls and Jeff had dates that night and invited Anna to join them, but she was tired and said she would like to just catch up on all the news with Aunt Helen. Anna dreaded the following day because she knew that she would be expected to go to church with the family. Once again, she was glad when church was over and came out feeling as though she had been attacked. The remainder of her time with the family passed very quickly with much genuine camaraderie and affection.

Wednesday morning she said goodbye to Uncle Ted and the girls as they left, and when Mr. Connors drove up, she kissed Aunt Helen on the cheek and hurried out to the car. She had enjoyed the visit and felt a little guilty to be so happy about returning to her job and the life she was building at the Burke's home. On the drive home Mr. Connors told her they had received a message the day before that the Burke's son Jason would be arriving Friday evening with two of his friends. Fortunately, Anna had cleaned all of the bedrooms before she left the week before, so they would only need to be touched up. When they arrived at the house and Mrs. Connors learned the rooms had all been cleaned the week before and would need only minimal work, she realized again what a blessing Anna was. By Thursday evening the entire house was ready and the only thing left was to prepare the Friday evening meal.

As soon as she could get away Wednesday evening, and then again Thursday evening, Anna went to sit beside the stream where she relaxed and watched the little people. She had been so caught up in the visit and earthly things she had not realized how much she missed the peace and serenity she found here. On Friday she went for a walk in the countryside where she met Tom. They talked for a while about her visit with her aunt's family and what had happened while she was gone, and then it was time for her to get back to help prepare dinner. As she returned to the house, she smiled at the thought of how everything had fallen into place so perfectly and how much at home she felt here.

Dinner was ready to be served and everything in order when they heard a car come up the drive and stop out front. While Mr. Connors assisted the boys with their bags, Mrs. Connors inquired about serving dinner and was told they would be ready in 30 minutes. Jason and his friends laughed and talked about college throughout dinner and teased Mrs. Connors about being such a good cook they would need help to get up from the table. It was obvious that Jason was fond of the couple that had worked for his family so long. He asked about Anna, and Mrs. Connors introduced her to Jason who in turn introduced her to his friends. After dinner the boys went into the parlor for after dinner drinks and to play games while Anna and Mrs. Connors cleaned the kitchen and dining room.

The following day Mr. and Mrs. Burke returned home, and Saturday Anna and Mrs. Connors were kept very busy fixing three meals a day for the Burkes and the three boys as well as cleaning all of the bedrooms. As usual the main Sunday meal had been prepared on Saturday, so once breakfast was served and the kitchen put to rights Anna was free to do as she pleased. She had already missed church, so she decided to go for a walk. Everyone was just leaving church as she passed, so she talked to Tom and the other young people for a while before continuing her walk. Of course she had taken her art supplies with her, so she walked until she came upon a lovely meadow where she sat down under a tree and was soon lost in her drawing. By the time she returned that afternoon the boys had left to return to school and things settled down again.

As Anna drifted off to sleep that night after thanking God for her wonderful life, she felt something brush across her cheeks as her parents kissed her goodnight.

Chapter 6

Anna was very happy with her life with the Burkes. She felt fortunate to be able to live in such beautiful surroundings and luxury and to be treated so well by everyone. Mrs. Burke was pleased with Anna's work and had given her a good raise, so Anna had more than enough for the few things she needed and was even able to save a little money each month.

She found time almost every day to slip away for a while and spend some time in the world of fairies and other creatures. The more time she spent with them, the more she was able to see and in time she was able to see all of the creatures including those like the little man who had opened the door for her the day she had stumbled upon the magical cottage. Her skill at recreating this world in pictures continued to grow, and in time the chalk and pencils were inadequate to satisfy her skills. On her next shopping trip she purchased watercolors in hopes of capturing the ethereal quality of this world. The following day was Sunday, and she was so eager to try her new supplies that she skipped church and went early into the open countryside where she could be alone. She worked diligently becoming more and more frustrated by her inability to capture the colors and dreamy nature of what she saw. As she worked a very short, strange looking man, much like the one that had opened the cottage door for her, spread out on the grass beside her to observe her efforts. She had never attempted to converse with any of the beings she saw, but it seemed rude to ignore him, so she looked at him and said hello. To her surprise, he answered. He stayed there throughout the day and did not speak much, but when she grew impatient with her inadequacy to capture what she saw, he told her to be patient, take a deep breath, and just let it happen. As she listened to his voice, she felt almost as though she stepped into the world of the little people and without effort began to sense on some deep level how to get the efforts she desired.

She jumped suddenly as she heard someone call her name and turned to find Tom standing there looking down at her. He asked if she was all right and said he had called her several times. He had come looking for her because she had not been at church, and he was concerned. Anna thanked him for his concern, apologized for causing him to worry and explained that she had been eager to try her new watercolors.

Tom looked over her shoulder at the picture and was transfixed by what he saw. It had such depth and seemed so real he felt as though he could step into the scene. This was very different from the picture she had been drawing the first day he met her, and he could not hide his surprise. They talked for a while about the picture, and she really wanted to share with him the truth about what she saw. However, she instinctively knew this would be a mistake as Tom was a good friend, but he was very down to earth and would never understand this. As they talked, he told her that she should take her pictures to market and sell them, and she laughed at the idea.

It was getting late, so Tom helped Anna gather everything and walked with her as far as the church where they said goodbye. She had not eaten since early that morning and suddenly realized she was ravenous. When she entered the kitchen, Mrs. Connors looked up with obvious relief, and Anna apologized explaining that she had gotten so caught up with her painting she lost track of time. Mrs. Connors asked to see her pictures, and Anna showed her the last three she had done. As Mrs. Connors looked at the three pictures, Anna put the earlier attempts into the stove and burned them. Mrs. Connors had seen other pictures Anna had done and knew that she was improving in skill, but she was as surprised as Tom had been when she saw what Anna had done today. The colors had been mixed to create such depth and beauty that they seemed to come to life. After that day each time Anna sat down to paint, the little man would come and lie down beside her while she worked, and she continued to improve under his influence.

The Burkes announced a few weeks later that they would be gone for the day. Anna had finished her work and was sitting in the kitchen having a cup of tea when Mr. Connors came in to ask if they needed anything as he was driving to town. Since Anna had finished her work, and they did not have to prepare dinner, she accompanied Mr. Connors while he did his errands in order to purchase some oils and canvasses.

It was toward the end of summer, but the days were still fairly long, so when they returned from town, Anna gathered her new art supplies and went to sit by the stream. It was twilight when she had her paints on the palette and began mixing colors. The little man came and sat beside her, and she began to paint as the full moon rose into the night sky. As usual, she became lost in her painting, and Mrs. Connors finally sent her husband to fetch her to come to bed because it was so late. Her first effort with oils was not as good as what she had achieved with watercolors, but it was still very good, and she set the canvas on her windowsill to dry.

As the days grew shorter, she worked more and more at night and was soon able to capture the special quality of light and color of the night. However, she made a point to stop painting earlier after that in order to avoid causing the Connors the trouble of coming to get her.

Chapter 7

Anna wrote to her Aunt Helen often but felt a little guilty that her life was so full she had little time for her family. It had been almost a year since her last visit when the Burkes announced on a Tuesday that they would be gone for a week beginning the following Wednesday. Anna wrote a hasty note to her aunt telling her that she could come the following Friday for a short visit and received a reply that week urging her to come. Anna worked very hard getting all her work done, and on Friday morning when Mr. Connors drove to town to do the errands, he dropped Anna at her aunt's home. Aunt Helen met Anna at the door with a big hug and led her to the kitchen where they sat down to talk about all that had happened since they had last seen each other.

Tom and the Connors had urged Anna to take her paintings to market, and she had decided that while she was in town with her aunt might be a good time to do that. She had mentioned to Aunt Helen that she spent a lot of her spare time painting, so after they had caught up on all the news she brought up the subject of trying to sell some of her paintings. While they talked about this, Anna unwrapped the paintings she had brought with her and set them up around the room. She became aware that her aunt had stopped talking and turned to find her staring at the paintings in amazement. When Anna had told her she did painting in her spare time, Helen had never imagined her niece was so talented.

The paintings were a mixture of watercolors and oils, and in the months since Anna had begun to work with these mediums her work had taken on an ethereal quality unmatched by anything her aunt had ever seen. They were still discussing the paintings when Stella, Ruth and Joan got home,

and Uncle Ted arrived about five minutes later. During dinner they talked
about the pictures and Aunt Helen explained Anna had brought them in
hopes of selling some at market. Everyone agreed that was a great idea,
and they made plans to all go to the market on Saturday to help Anna with
this. Anna had brought 14 paintings of different sizes, and she told Aunt
Helen to choose one as a gift. She was very pleased when Aunt Helen chose
a night scene of the tiny fairies dancing at the edge of the water, as that was
one of Anna's favorites. Anna longed to talk to them and tell them that
this world was real, but she knew that her family, like Tom, would never
understand. The lack of someone to share her secret world was the one
regret she had about her life.

After dinner, they all helped put price tags on the paintings. Anna had no
idea what to charge but was sure the price Uncle Ted suggested as too high;
however, they agreed they could always come down if necessary. On Saturday
morning they all piled into the car with Anna's paintings and set out for the
market. Even though they got there early, the market was very crowded. They
finally found a small area and drove the sticks they had brought to support
the paintings into the ground and leaned the paintings against them. There
was soon a group of people gathered around the paintings, and Anna blushed
as she heard them talk about how wonderful they were. Within a couple of
hours, all of the paintings had been sold except two small watercolors and
Anna's head was swimming. The people had not hesitated to pay the prices
on the painting, and Anna had never seen so much money before.

Since there were only two paintings left, the family decided to wander
around for a while and left Anna alone. Almost immediately a middle-aged
woman approached and began looking at the two remaining pictures. Anna
was caught off guard when the woman looked her in the eye and asked
if she saw the things she painted. She was too stunned to answer at once,
but as they looked into each other's eyes she knew that she could tell the
truth and answered yes. The woman asked Anna's name and introduced
herself as Lilith. She asked if Anna had always had this gift and listened
intently as Anna told her about the day her mother died.

As they talked, a few people stopped to look at the paintings and a
small, elderly lady in a funny little hat bought the picture of an elf sitting
on a rock by the stream. They both laughed when Lilith remarked that the
woman looked a lot like the elf. Anna explained that she was the maid for a
family outside of town and had little free time, but that she was very happy.
It seemed only moments before the family was back, and Lilith introduced
herself telling them that she had a small gallery in town and was interested
in selling Anna's paintings. She gave Anna her card and told her to bring
any paintings she had to her gallery whenever she was in town, and she
bought the one remaining painting.

Anna insisted on taking them all out to dinner that night to celebrate, and they had a wonderful time. Even though it was late when they got to bed, Anna was sure she couldn't sleep because she was so excited; however, she fell asleep almost immediately and dreamed of being with her mother and father in a place much like those in her paintings.

The next morning being Sunday Anna accompanied the family to church where she let her mind wander remembering the day before and thinking about Lilith. She felt a little guilty but smiled to herself as she realized that this was the first time she had not been miserable there.

Once again, Anna said goodbye to the girls and Uncle Ted as they left the next morning, and then she and Aunt Helen sat down to have a cup of tea while they waited for Mr. Connors to arrive. They talked about Anna's mother, and laughed at stories Aunt Helen told her about Anna's mother and her as young girls. Anna felt very close to Aunt Helen, and as they said goodbye, she was truly glad she had come and wished she could stay longer.

Mr. Connors noticed that Anna had no paintings left, and she told him she had sold all of them except the one she gave to Aunt Helen. When they arrived home, Mrs. Connors had lunch ready, and they sat down to eat while Anna told them about her visit and the trip to the market. They were impressed and congratulated her when she showed them the card Lilith had given her and told them about the offer to sell her paintings in Lilith's gallery.

On her next shopping trip, Anna spent some of the money that she had gotten for her paintings to purchase better quality paints, brushes and canvases. She was still amazed at how readily people had spent so much money to buy her paintings, but she never thought about money when she was painting because she got so caught up in the life of her subjects.

Anna often wondered about the little people she painted, and one day when the little man had joined her, she asked him to tell her about the little people. He explained that there were many different groups and they each had a specific purpose. She asked which group he belonged to, and he said he was what humans called a gnome. He pointed out others and told her about them, and she said she had always been told none of these really existed. The gnome explained this was because humans had broken the ties with all of the elementals long ago. The elementals are responsible for caring for the earth and in the beginning when humans were closely tied to the earth and worked with the elementals they could see them. However, once humans stopped caring for the earth and began to exploit and destroy it, they lost the ability to see the elementals and to have their help. Now the elementals spent all of their time trying to reverse the damage done by humans. He grew very angry as he talked about how selfish humans were and how much damage they did through their ignorance.

Anna had wondered why she could see them and others could not. When she asked the gnome about this, he told her that she had been given the gift because she had a pure heart, and it would help her fulfill her destiny. This really intrigued her, but when she asked what he meant by her destiny, he simply stated that she had been led to where she needed to be, and it was up to her to proceed. She kept asking for more information about this, but he would not answer and finally told her he had said too much already and would have to leave if she continued to ask questions. After that day, Anna often talked to the gnome and others as she painted them, but she asked no more questions about herself. She still did not understand why she was given the gift to see them but certainly didn't want to risk losing it.

During the summer break from college, the Burkes' son Jason was home for a month before going to visit a friend at the seashore. Two of his friends came to stay for short visits while he was home, and with more people in the house there was a lot more work to do. This left little time for Anna to paint, but since the days were long, she had some time most evenings and on Sunday. She continued to attend dances and other events with Tom and the other young people and often saw one of them on Sunday afternoons when she gathered her supplies and went in search of a subject to paint.

Anna often thought about Lilith and wished she could take some of her paintings to Lilith's gallery and see her again, but there was no opportunity to get away. One day she was going through her paintings and decided to get rid of some of the earliest ones because they were so crude compared to what she was doing now. She bundled them up and had started outside to put them in the rubbish when Mrs. Connors asked what she was doing. She explained that she was taking them out to be burned and Mrs. Connors asked if she could see them and began to spread the paintings out on the large kitchen table. Mrs. Burke entered the kitchen to discuss the menu for that week and upon seeing the paintings asked where they had come from. Mrs. Connors explained that Anna had painted them but was going to destroy them because she didn't considered them to be very good.

Mrs. Burke asked Anna about this and was told that these were early works, and she did much better now. At Mrs. Burke's request, she went to her room and returned with several of her later paintings, which she placed on the table with the others. Mrs. Burke stated that, although the later pictures were better, the earlier paintings were good and asked if she could have the ones Anna was going to destroy to sell for a charity auction she was involved in. Anna happily agreed, and the three of them took the paintings to Mrs. Burke's car.

Chapter 8

As the days grew shorter, it became more difficult to find time to paint, and she began taking her sketchpad and pencil with her to do a quick sketch and then painted in her room at night by the fire. Fall quickly turned to winter, and as the holidays approached the work increased. Jason was home for Thanksgiving and again for two weeks at Christmas, and Mrs. Burke told them just after Thanksgiving that she would be having a party for 150 people in two weeks.

Because Anna kept the house in very good shape, it wasn't necessary to have any help until two days before the party. Anna, and Mr. and Mrs. Connors began decorating for Christmas the day after Thanksgiving. She had never seen such splendid decorations and enjoyed working long hours to get everything perfect. Finally, three days before the party the decorating was done, and they had one day before they had to begin baking and preparing food for the party. Mrs. Burke had hired a local girl to help out, and they were all very tired by the time everything was ready the day before the party. The night of the party the house looked like a fairy tale palace with every room decorated and ablaze with light and every fireplace with a fire burning brightly. The party lasted until two in the morning and it was three before they all got to bed even though they had kept up with the clearing all night. Mrs. Burke complimented them on how well they had done and told them not to worry about breakfast the following morning.

When Anna awoke, the sun was high overhead, and she heard Mr. and Mrs. Connors talking in the kitchen. The fire in her room was out, so she shivered as she dressed quickly and hurried to the kitchen where a warm fire was already burning in the stove. They sat talking about the people at the party, how beautiful the women's dresses were, how handsome the men looked and what a wonderful time everyone had seemed to have. It was afternoon before the Burkes rose for the day. They had cleaned the downstairs and Mrs. Burke told them not to worry about the upstairs that day but to just fix a light lunch and then take the rest of the day off.

It had snowed during the night, and everything sparkled in the bright sunlight. Anna dressed warmly and set out across the white expanse with her sketchpad. As she trudged through the deep snow, she saw the little people in the clearings under trees and in sheltered areas dancing and celebrating the beauty of the season. She made a few sketches and then started back home. The sun had set and the landscape looked as though it had been sprinkled with jewels as the full moon reflected off the snow and ice. She shivered as she retraced her steps to the warm kitchen where Mrs. Connors offered her a cup of hot tea. The night was very cold, and they were all still tired, so after having a simple dinner and cleaning the kitchen, they retired to their rooms. That night Anna dreamed of being in a crystal castle that reflected all the colors of the rainbow with people who seemed to be all dressed in white and glowing as if from within.

After the party, life got back to its usual routine except that the cold kept them indoors a lot more than before. Mrs. Connors showed Anna a throw she had knitted as a gift for the Burkes, and Anna brought out a painting she had done of the house to ask if the Connors thought it would be suitable to give to the Burkes. It was a fairly small painting, but she had managed to catch the brilliance of the trees and plants resplendent in their fall colors and everything awash with the fiery pink glow of the setting sun. Mr. And Mrs. Connors said they felt it would be a splendid gift, and Mr. Connors offered to frame the painting as his gift.

Anna and the Connors had planned to attend midnight mass on Christmas Eve, but the snow had been so heavy they decided not to risk it. Christmas day was very cold, and the world outside looked like a wonderland of diamonds with the sunlight reflecting off the icicles and snow. As they worked preparing breakfast and Mr. Connors laid and started fires, Anna thought how different this was from the Christmases she had spent with her mother and felt a lump come into her throat. Even though she was aware of her parents' presence and knew they were always with her, it was not the same as having them with her in the physical world. She longed to be able to lay her head in her mother's lap and feel her loving touch as she stroked her hair the way she had always done whenever Anna had been sad or hurt.

When breakfast had been served to the Burkes, Anna and Mr. and Mrs. Connors exchanged gifts while they ate their own breakfast. Mrs. Connors gave Anna a beautiful bag that she had made of heavy canvas large enough for Anna to carry all of her painting supplies in, and Mr. Connors had made her a short easel that she could use sitting or lying on the ground. She hugged both of them as she thanked them for the perfect, thoughtful gifts. She had bought a pair of warm gloves for Mr. Connors and a warm but delicate shawl for Mrs. Connors that she had found at the market on her last visit with her aunt.

After breakfast, Mrs. Burke called the three of them to come to the parlor where the family was getting ready to open gifts. As they entered the room, Mrs. Burke handed each of them their gift. Mrs. Connors gave Mrs. Burke her gift and Anna gave Mrs. Burke the gift-wrapped painting. They opened their gifts and both Mr. and Mrs. Connors had received a pair of very expensive, warm boots. Anna's gift was a book of famous painters and their works, and she thanked Mrs. Burke and told her she had never had anything so beautiful before. Mrs. Burke opened the package with the throw and immediately placed it on the back of the sofa where she often reclined to read. She told Mrs. Connors that she had often wished she had something to put over her as she read on cold nights. When she opened the painting she remarked about how beautiful Anna had made their home look and how proud they would be to hang the painting in a prominent spot for everyone to see. Anna explained that Mr. Connors had made the hand carved frame, and both Mr. Burke and Jason complimented Anna on her talent and Mr. Connors on his fine handiwork. None of them had noticed in the painting the little man who was peaking out from under a shrub at the front of the house.

It was obvious to Mrs. Burke that Anna was very talented, and she was torn between wanting to help her and not wanting to lose such a good maid. Several days later she overheard Anna telling Mrs. Connors that she wished she were able to visit with Lilith and take some of her paintings to the gallery. She asked Anna about this, and Anna explained that she had taken some paintings to the market to sell when she had visited her aunt and told her about meeting Lilith who offered to sell her paintings.

Mrs. Burke had been impressed by Anna's loyalty and hard work and decided she must help her even if it did mean losing a very good maid; therefore, she told Anna that if she had all of her work caught up for the week Mr. Connors could drive her to the gallery on Friday. Anna became so excited she could barely keep from hugging Mrs. Burke as she thanked her with tears in her eyes. For the rest of the week Anna hummed as she worked extra hard getting all of the work done, and on Friday she had everything finished by the time Mr. Connors returned after dropping Mr. Burke at work. Although he normally did his errands before returning home, Mrs. Burke had told Mr. Connors to return for Anna and drop her off at the gallery while he took care of his errands and then pick her up when he started back home.

Chapter 9

All week Anna had worried that Lilith would not be there or she would have changed her mind or something, and when they reached the gallery, she nervously went inside. Lilith looked up as the bell on the door tinkled merrily to announce someone's arrival and smiled on seeing Anna standing very uncertainly in the doorway. She hurried over, gave Anna a hug, told her she was glad to see her and asked if she had brought any paintings. Anna told her she had brought 16 paintings, and they both went to the car where Anna introduced Lilith to Mr. Connors, who helped carry in the paintings and told Anna he would not be back for at least three hours.

Lilith spread the paintings out and stood looking at them without saying a word, but as she moved from one to another she made little sounds that Anna could not be sure were approval or disapproval. Finally, Lilith turned to Anna and told her these paintings were far better than she had expected, and they would bring very good prices. Anna couldn't imagine that they would sell for more than the others had and was stunned when Lilith told her what she was going to ask for them. Anna had never been in a gallery before, and Lilith gave her a tour explaining the different styles and techniques to her and pointing out little tricks and things that made the paintings special. After about 30 minutes she ushered Anna to the back of the gallery where there was a small kitchen and invited her to sit as she fixed them a cup of tea, and they talked about the paintings and the little people.

As they sipped their tea, Lilith asked what Anna did in the evenings and on Sundays when she was off, and Anna told her about going to church and to local dances and gatherings. They talked about Tom and the other young people she had met and about church, and Anna told Lilith about going to her aunt's church and how bad it made her feel. Lilith told Anna she had experienced the same kind of feelings and then told her a little about the church she attended. She explained that in her church they were open to people of different backgrounds and beliefs and embraced a belief in astrology, reincarnation, and many other things that were often frowned upon by other churches. Anna said she wished she were able to attend this church because it sounded fascinating and more like what she thought a church should be. Anna enjoyed her visit with Lilith and was surprised when Mr. Connors came into the gallery to learn how much time had passed. As they said goodbye, Anna promised to return when she could and bring some more paintings.

Anna hurried to get to church early Sunday, as she was eager to tell Tom about her visit with Lilith. She and Tom had become very good friends and often spent evenings and Sunday afternoons together. They talked for a while before church started, and she was disappointed that Tom did not share her excitement. She was unaware that Tom's feelings for her had become much more than just those of a friend, and that he resented her being so preoccupied with her painting. He was also concerned about what it would mean for them if she were successful. There was a dance the following Saturday, and as usual they agreed to meet at the church even though they would almost surely see each other at some time during the coming week.

The weather had begun to warm in anticipation of spring and after church, Anna packed her painting supplies and new easel in her new bag. The bag made it much easier to carry everything, and she kept a good pace happy to be out in the open again. She had always walked in the direction of the church and decided to try a different direction. She knew from talking to others that the countryside was deserted to the north, and she had avoided this for fear of becoming lost. Now that she was more familiar with the area, she felt it was time to take a chance. She had walked perhaps two miles when she topped a rise and looked down on a grassy meadow with a clear pool and a small waterfall. She laughed at herself as she stumbled and almost fell into the pool in her eagerness to unpack her painting supplies and get started. The gnome that usually kept her company when she painted did not appear, and Anna realized she missed his company. She looked around for a subject to paint and saw that there was a community of little people just to her left under a large willow tree. The willow limbs created an ever-shifting curtain that lent an air of mystery as it offered glimpses of what was behind it, and she decided this would be a very interesting picture.

As usual, Anna quickly became lost in her painting and was startled when catching movement out of the corner of her eye she looked up to see a beautiful angel with translucent wings standing at the edge of the pool smiling at her. She had become accustomed to seeing the little people and had come to accept them as part of her world. However, she was startled by the angel that appeared to be surrounded by a shimmering light of beautiful, pulsing colors and was like the figures she had dreamt of in the crystal castle. The angel slowly disappeared, and Anna shook her head wondering if she had only imagined it.

She returned to her painting and worked until the shadow of the tree made her realize that it would soon be dark, and she shivered as a chill crept into the air. She gathered everything together and struggled up the hill with her load. When she reached the top, she turned to take one last look and caught her breath as the angel appeared once more by the pool and smiled. Anna smiled in return and turned to hurry home before dark for fear of losing her way.

That night she lay in bed wondering why she had suddenly seen the angel today and never before. As she drifted off to sleep, she once again heard the now familiar small voice whisper, "Because you are moving toward something new and wonderful."

As the weather grew warmer and the evenings longer, Anna wandered farther into areas she had never been, but she often returned to the glade where she had seen the angel because she found no other place as special. With spring the flowers burst into bloom and nature seemed to be celebrating the end of winter. The birds were singing and the little people rushed around laughing and dancing well into the night. She had painted for a while at the glade one warm spring afternoon when she suddenly put down her brushes and stretched out lazily in the grass. She was drifting somewhere between waking and sleep when she noticed a tall figure coming toward her. It was surrounded with the same light as the angel she had seen before, and she felt no fear as the being came and sat beside her. The being appeared to be neither male nor female but a blending of both, and as she was enfolded in its light, she felt a love and joy so intense that it was almost painful. She looked up into eyes that were a brilliant violet color and suddenly began to hear the being; although, the lips never moved. She realized that she was hearing the thoughts as the being told her of another world that was in this same place but because it was a different vibration most of the time humans are unaware of it. She had started to ask a question when the being answered her, and she realized that the being heard her thoughts as well. They sat for a long time communicating in this special way while the being explained about death and that each of us comes here many times until we finally reach a state where we can rejoin the source from which we came.

Finally, the being told Anna it was time to go and she realized that it was indeed getting very late. The being moved away, and she began packing her things to go home. As she looked around, she realized that the little people had grown very quiet and were looking at the shining being with an attitude of reverence. When she looked back, the being had disappeared, and she picked up her things and made her way to the top of the hill. As usual, when she reached the top she turned and looked back at the glade. This time, she saw her mother and father standing together by the pool smiling at her. She smiled and turned to make her way home. On the walk home she was lost in thought wondering what was happening. She wished she were able to talk to someone about this and share the wonder of it, but she knew there was no one here she could talk to. Once again, she found herself longing to visit Lilith, as she sensed this was the one person she knew who could help her understand.

Chapter 10

One Saturday afternoon Anna returned from a walk to help serve dinner and upon approaching the house noticed there was a strange car in the drive. She hurried to the kitchen in case Mrs. Connors needed her help and stopped short as Lilith looked up from the table where she was sitting talking to Mrs. Connors. Anna smiled and ran to give Lilith a hug, as she told her how much she had been wishing she could see her.

Lilith explained that she has sold most of Anna's paintings and took an envelope out of her purse, which she handed to Anna stating it was the money for the paintings she had sold. Anna opened the envelope and saw that it was filled with bills, so many that she thought she was going to faint as she began counting the money, and Lilith suggested she might want to open an account at a bank to keep the money in. Mrs. Connors told Anna she was sure Mrs. Burke would agree to let her ride with Mr. Connors when he went into town so that she could open the account, and Lilith, realizing Anna probably did not know how to open an account, explained that all she had to do was go into the bank and tell one of the people behind the counter that she wanted to open a savings account.

They talked while Anna and Mrs. Connors finished preparing dinner, and Anna brought out paintings for Lilith to look at. As she studied the paintings, Lilith realized that Anna had continued to grow not only in her skill but in other areas as well. When she picked up the painting Anna had done of the angel at the pool, Anna protested saying she had been unable to get it the way she wanted, and Lilith assured her it was wonderful. Anna had started including seemingly empty landscapes, but as Lilith looked closely she saw that there was always at least one of the little people somewhere in the paintings.

When Anna served the first course, Mrs. Burke stated she thought she had heard a strange voice and asked if someone else was in the kitchen. Anna apologized as she explained that the lady who owned the gallery had come to get some more paintings, and Mrs. Burke assured Anna that it was all right and she should invite the lady to join her for dinner. Anna returned to the kitchen and extended Mrs. Burke's invitation to Lilith who said she would love to join them because everything looked and smelled wonderful. They all fixed their plates and ate while Anna and Mrs. Connors took turns serving the Burkes. They had finished eating when Mrs. Burke entered the kitchen and introduced herself to Lilith, and Anna realized that Mrs. Burke considered her friend an equal as Lilith and Mrs. Burke chatted about acquaintances they had in common.

Lilith thanked Mrs. Burke for her hospitality and said she had to get back home before it grew too late. She told Anna she wanted to take all the paintings, and they carried them out to her car. Anna was very disappointed that she and Lilith had not had any time to talk privately, but as they said goodbye Lilith hugged her and assured her that they would have time alone when the time was right.

The following Monday Anna rode to town with Mr. Connors and opened an account while he did his errands. He had told her he would be back in an hour and a half and since she had an hour to wait, she decided to just look in some of the shops while she waited. She had kept out some of the money to buy more supplies, and she thought she might find something different since this was not where she usually shopped for her supplies. As she walked down the street, she passed a small shop that had beautiful stones, books, and many interesting things in the window. She entered the shop and noticed that a very nice fragrance filled the air and saw an elderly lady behind the counter dressed in unusual clothing that draped in layers with flowers and birds painted in bright colors all over it. She asked about the fragrance, and the lady told her it was incense and showed her the different types and fragrances.

Anna felt as though she had stepped into another world as she looked around the shop. There were books on a great variety of subjects that Anna knew nothing about but that sounded very interesting, many strange stones in various shapes and sizes, clothing like that worn by the lady, decks of cards and many other unusual things that Anna could not begin to understand. As the lady watched Anna with interest, she could tell that Anna did not understand most of what she saw, but she knew there was a reason for her being there and did not interfere. Anna had turned to leave when she saw a small statue of a gnome that looked very much like the one who had stayed with her when she painted, and she decided to buy it to remind her of him since she had not seen him for quite some time. She also decided to buy some of the incense and a small purple stone that she had kept coming back to and felt compelled to keep picking up. This was the first time Anna had ever been able to buy something just because she wanted it, and she was still not comfortable with the idea.

She had barely exited the shop when Mr. Connors arrived to take her back home. On the way home she told him about opening the account and how nice everyone had been to her. She then told him about the strange little shop she had discovered and the lady who ran it and showed him the things she had bought. Mr. Connors really cared for Anna, but he sometimes wondered if she might be a little balmy, and he worried that she would go completely over the edge with these things that she painted and now spending money on such foolishness. He thought it was probably because she spent too much time alone and wished she would find a nice boy and settle down and get married.

Chapter 11

The following Saturday there was a party at the church, and Anna and Tom arranged to meet there as usual. Anna enjoyed being with the young people, but it seemed that she didn't have a lot to talk about with them, as she dared not talk about those things that were becoming more and more important to her. She and Tom wandered outside with a cool drink and sat down on a bench. They could hear the music and laughter from inside, but it all seemed far away. Tom looked at Anna in the soft light from the window and realized that he loved her very much and wanted to spend the rest of his life with her. He reached out and took her hand, and she closed her eyes as he gently kissed her on the lips. She felt warm and safe with Tom and wondered if this was what love was really like and not the all-consuming passion that she had read about. They sat with Tom's arm around her shoulders and talked quietly until the party was over and everyone started to leave.

Tom told her he had loved her for a long time and wanted her to be his wife. He talked about someday having a small farm of his own and said he wanted to have at least three or four children, because he had been an only child and always wished he had brothers and sisters. As Anna listened to him talk about his dreams for the future, a part of her wanted this perfect life while another part of her wanted to run away. Deep within her she felt as if there was something important that was waiting for her even though she didn't know what it was. Tom walked her home that night and kissed her gently on the lips again as he said goodnight. She lay awake for a long time wondering what it was that life held for her and wishing she could talk to her mother. She finally fell asleep and dreamed of being locked in a dark, dreary room and looking out a window at a beautiful world, which she longed to explore. She awoke with a deep sense of sadness and longing and knew she had to tell Tom that she did not love him.

Mrs. Connors noticed the next day that Anna seemed very quiet and a little sad and asked if something had upset her. Anna told Mrs. Connors about Tom saying he loved her and wanted to marry her, and Mrs. Connors said that was wonderful, but what did it have to do with her being sad. Anna explained that she did not love Tom and had to tell him because it would be cruel to lead him on. Mr. Connors had come in while they talked, and while he normally tried not to interfere in someone else's life, he could not control himself this time. He told Anna she must be daft to even consider turning down such a fine young man as Tom for some silly business about love. Anna and Mrs. Connors stood in stunned silence as Mr. Connors turned and stormed out of the kitchen after his outburst. Mrs. Connors talked to Anna and assured her that real love was not at all what you read about in books and that the important thing was having respect for someone and knowing that they would be there through good times and bad. What Mrs. Connors said made sense, and Anna really did care for Tom, so she decided not to say anything for now and just see what happened.

Tom started coming over every afternoon just as Anna would be getting ready to go for a walk and do some painting, and staying until after dinner. She found that even though she could see the little people, she was unable to paint them with Tom there, and he seemed to resent anything that took her attention from him. A few times she told him that she really would like to just be alone, but it was as though he didn't even hear her. She began to feel the way she had felt in the dream, and the thought of spending the rest of her life like this was unbearable. After about a month, she made up her mind that the next time he came over she would make him understand that she needed time alone to do her painting and just be quiet.

The next day Tom arrived just as she had hung the last of the laundry on the line. She was free until the laundry was dry, so they walked down to the small stream behind the house, and she began to explain how she felt. She knew that he really cared for her and didn't want to hurt him, but she felt as though she were being smothered. Tom became very angry and said that he wanted to be with her because he loved her, and she must not love him at all if she couldn't stand to be with him. She tried again to explain, but he just ranted and raved and wouldn't let her talk at all. Finally, she became angry and looking him straight in the eye told him that she didn't love him and had no intention of spending the rest of her life with him the way he was acting. At that Tom turned and walked away without even saying goodbye.

This was Anna's first experience with raw, hateful anger, and she was so upset that she began crying from the stress and frustration. She had been taught never to say something that she knew would hurt someone else, and she was shocked at herself and Tom for being so cruel. She sat by the stream for a long time feeling dejected and lonely. Suddenly, she became aware that she was no longer alone and turning saw the gnome stretched out on the grass beside her. She very curtly asked what he was doing here now when he had not been around for such a long time. The gnome quietly answered that he had been there for her originally to give her encouragement in her painting, and that he had come back today because he thought she needed a friend. At this Anna began to really cry large gulping sobs and told him how much she had missed his company. She even told him about buying the small statue of a gnome that looked a lot like him to remind her of him. They sat for a while longer just watching the water in the stream as it bubbled and tumbled its way downstream. Suddenly Anna realized she was no longer upset and unhappy and thanked the gnome for being her friend and helping her. It was time to get back and finish with the laundry, so she rose, said goodbye and started toward the house.

When she entered the kitchen, Mrs. Connors asked if Tom was staying for dinner and was told he had left. Mrs. Connors could tell that something was wrong, but she decided it would be best to let Anna tell her what it was in her own time. That night as they ate dinner, Anna told Mr. and Mrs. Connors that she and Tom had an argument and had broken up. Mr. Connors didn't say anything, but she could tell he didn't approve. Mrs. Connors, however, had seen how domineering Tom had become and had begun to wonder if he was really such a good choice. She was not surprised at the news and realized she was even somewhat relieved.

The next afternoon when Anna had finished the daily cleaning, Mrs. Connors told her that the Burkes would not be home for dinner, so she could have the rest of the day off. Anna packed her painting supplies and started out for a walk and suddenly realized she felt very free and happy. She had not been to the glade where she had seen the angel for a long time and decided to go there. When she reached the top of the rise, she stopped for a moment to drink in the beauty and peace of the place. The walk had been quite long, and it was a warm afternoon, so she decided to get a drink of water from the pool. As she sat on the bank close to the water, spray from the waterfall covered her with a light mist. She closed her eyes and sat listening to the sound of the water, the little people under the willow tree, the birds and all the wonderful sounds of nature.

After a few minutes, Anna rose and returned to where she had everything laid out and began to mix paints. She looked toward the waterfall and saw the faint image of a woman in the water coming over the fall. She also noticed that there were hundreds of balls of brilliant light floating through the air all around her and decided to paint this scene. She painted until the light had completely faded and then realizing how late it was hurriedly packed everything and walked quickly home in the gathering darkness. Mrs. Connors looked up in obvious relief when she entered the kitchen. Anna apologized for being so late and said she was really hungry as she had not eaten anything since lunch.

Anna placed the painting she had done on a table in her room, and she looked at it often in the coming weeks. It seemed to have a depth and life that none of her other paintings had, and she realized that she had been totally caught up in it when she was painting. She wondered what the balls of light were and sensed that they had significance.

She talked to Tom after church a couple of weeks after the argument, and he said he wanted to be friends. Even though he was hurt, he admitted it was good that Anna had been honest with him about her feelings. During the following weeks, Anna realized that she was lonely for someone to share things with. Even though her relationship with Tom had been far from perfect, it had made her realize that something was missing in her life.

Chapter 12

Anna had been with the Burkes for more than a year, when Mrs. Burke told her that they would be taking a vacation in a month and Anna could have a full week off during that time. Of course, Anna wrote immediately to Aunt Helen and received a note of invitation to visit with them. She also wrote to Lilith who invited her to spend a few days with her and asked that she bring any paintings she had. Anna decided to spend the first four days with the family and the last three days with Lilith and wrote giving them the dates.

There was a lot of work to do getting everything ready for the Burkes' trip, so the month was gone almost before Anna knew it. The Burkes left on Wednesday to be gone for two weeks, so Anna decided to start her vacation the following week, and on the Saturday evening following the Burkes' departure, Mr. Connors drove Anna to her aunt's house. Anna told him that Lilith would pick her up at her Aunt's home on Wednesday and then drive her home at the end of her vacation.

Anna, of course, accompanied the family to church the following day, but she knew what to expect now, and it did not seem so bad. She spent the time enjoying the beautiful windows and architecture of the building. After church, they all went for a picnic in a park not far from Aunt Helen's house where they played games and enjoyed each other's company. Anna had never played games much because there had been little time growing up and very few playmates. They were all patient with her as she learned the different games, and she felt very close to this family she had not known until recently.

Joan and Ruth were both working now and were seriously dating and thinking about marriage. Jeff had a new girlfriend but did not seem too serious, as he had been quite hurt by the last girl. Even little Stella had a boyfriend. When they asked Anna about her boyfriend, she said they were only friends, and she did not have a boyfriend. They told her all that had happened since her last visit. Anna told them about going to Lilith's gallery and Lilith bringing the money to her and getting more paintings. She proudly showed them the savings book that Lilith had told her to bring because she had more money for her to put in while she was in town, but she did not discuss the things that she and Lilith talked about other than art. Anna had brought paintings with her, and they all complimented her as they spread the paintings around the room to get a good look at them. They teased her a lot about her subjects, and Jeff said he had better try to find her a boyfriend before it was too late. Aunt Helen picked up the painting of the figure in the waterfall and remarked that Anna's talent had developed a lot, and they all agreed.

Listening to them all talk about their lives made Anna feel sad as she thought about her mother and how unfair it seemed that she had lost both her parents and been left alone so young. She often found herself longing to be able to talk to her mother about those things a girl can only discuss with her mother. That night she dreamt that she was back in the glade, and the being of light told her that she had lost her parents because she had a very important purpose in life, which she could not have done if she had stayed where she was. She asked what this purpose was, and the being told her that she was already doing what she was supposed to do for now and the rest would come at the right time. The being left, and her mother and father came and held her in their arms while they talked to her about how much she would do to help others and how important her purpose in life was. Anna asked why she had to have a purpose and said she would rather have them and be happy. They explained that everyone has a purpose but most never realize it and few have the potential Anna had for achieving something wonderful. They assured her that she would be happy and would not always be alone, and with that they each kissed her on the cheek and faded away.

Anna enjoyed her visit with the family very much but was eager to spend some time with Lilith. They had arranged for Lilith to pick her up after dinner Wednesday evening, and the entire family was there to say goodbye when it was time to leave. They all filed outside carrying the paintings Anna had brought and stood waving as she rode away with Lilith after much hugging and tears.

Lilith drove to the gallery to drop off the paintings, and they spent some time discussing them as they placed them out of harm's way. Lilith spent quite a while looking at the painting of the figure in the waterfall and smiled as she realized Anna was indeed ready to be exposed to deeper truths. She had planned to stop for dinner at her favorite restaurant on the way home and asked if Anna would mind, which of course Anna said she would not. When they reached the restaurant, Lilith was greeted by almost everyone there and introduced Anna to them explaining that Anna had painted many of the beautiful pictures they had seen in her gallery.

Anna was accustomed to meals of plain, hearty foods and the foods they were served were very different. There was a variety of fruits and vegetables covered in thin, delicate sauces and small pieces of meat lightly seasoned and cooked over an open flame, so that it was seared on the outside and juicy inside. All of this was served on a bed of rice with a thin, dark sauce that Lilith warned her was quite salty, so she should use only a small amount.

They sat at a large table with about 15 other people, and Anna found the conversation very confusing but fascinating. The talk concerned how things that were happening were determined by the position of stars and their relationship to each other and how these things impacted different people depending on their horoscope. Anna had read references to astrology and found it very interesting, but this subject had been considered evil, so she had always been afraid of it. They also talked about messages that people received, and this really confused Anna because she could not understand how these messages were received or where they came from.

The lady sitting to Anna's right introduced herself as Donna and asked Anna if she had painted the pictures of the little people. When Anna answered yes, Donna said Lilith had told them that she saw the beings she painted. Anna looked at Lilith who smiled and told her it was okay to talk to her friends about what she saw and heard. Everyone began asking questions, and Anna explained about the first time she had seen the beings and told them the story of the cottage. There were discussions about seeing things, how different people felt when this happened and about dreams and how important they are. Anna could have stayed all night talking to these people who were so interesting and who seemed eager to answer her questions, but it was getting late. Lilith told her they really had to go but assured her she would see everyone again.

From outside, Lilith's house looked very large, but when Lilith unlocked the front door, Anna was surprised to find herself in a courtyard with a long pool down the center and masses of flowers and trees filling the air with perfume. What she had thought was the walls of a house were actually walls with a roof over walkways around the courtyard. Anna followed Lilith as she turned to the left and entered a small building. Anna looked around and saw that there was a small kitchen to the right, with a small table with four chairs and a sofa, chair and two tables filling the rest of the room. Straight ahead and to the left she could see a large bed in another room and two doors to the right. The furniture was very simple but looked comfortable, and there were flowers in vases on the tables. They walked into the room at the back and placed Anna's bags on the floor. Lilith showed her where there were clean towels, a robe and the closet where she could hang her things.

Lilith then asked Anna to come with her to the main house for a cup of tea before they went to bed. They walked across a small bridge that crossed the pool and Lilith slid a glass door to the side and entered into the main room. She explained that her bedroom and bath were to the right and through the kitchen and dining room on the left was another bedroom and bath. All of the walls of the main room and kitchen and dining room that faced the courtyard were glass and large doors could be slid sideways so that the rooms were open to the outdoors. There were dim lights throughout the courtyard and Lilith turned on very soft lights in the main room. She also turned music on very low that was so beautiful it stirred something deep within Anna and almost made her want to cry. They took their cups of tea and sat on a sofa that faced the courtyard and listened to the music, night sounds and the sound of wind chimes as they were stirred by a gentle breeze.

Anna asked about the tea and was told that it was made from herbs that had a calming, soothing effect. She laughed and said if she got anymore relaxed she would be asleep, and Lilith suggested they probably should get to bed. They finished their tea and then walked to the doorway where Anna thanked Lilith and told her how much she had enjoyed the evening. As Anna walked back across the bridge, she looked around and saw that the courtyard was filled with fairies, and a variety of little people including a few gnomes and leprechauns. She ran water in the tub and slipped into the water. There were many bottles of shampoo and scents on a shelf by the tub and she poured some scent into the water from a bottle that was labeled lavender. The lather from the soap felt like silk against her skin, and she felt like she had been transported to a wonderland of luxury. After shampooing and rinsing her hair, she stepped from the tub in a perfumed haze and dried on a soft, thick towel. She put on her gown and slipped between the sheets in the large bed. The bed supported her weight but was incredibly soft, and her eyes grew heavy and closed almost as soon as her head touched the scented pillow as she burrowed beneath the billowy cover.

Anna awoke early the next morning feeling more alive than she had ever felt. It was still dark, when she slipped on the robe that was hanging in the bathroom and went to sit outside in the early morning dew and listen to the sound of the world as it woke for the day. The little people were starting to stir, and she watched them as they went about their work and play. As she leaned back against the tree behind the bench, she began to feel a pulsing coming from it and felt as though she were merging with the tree. She could feel the roots reaching deep into the dark, moist earth and the limbs stretching upward to the sky, and as she closed her eyes, she became aware of everything around her in a way that she had never been before.

Lilith stood in the doorway watching Anna until she saw her begin to stir and then walked toward her. Anna had a strange look on her face, and Lilith asked her if anything was wrong. Anna told her what she had felt and that she had never experienced anything like that before. Lilith explained that everything is alive and if we try we can connect with that life force. They rose and went inside where Lilith told her that breakfast was almost ready. They had hard-boiled eggs and very thin pancakes covered with fruit, sauce and whipped cream, which Lilith explained were called crepes. They laughed and talked while they ate and Anna remarked how good this was and that she was going to be very spoiled by the time she returned home.

After breakfast they returned to their rooms to dress as Lilith had invited Anna to spend the day with her at the gallery. At the gallery, they worked getting Anna's paintings ready to hang and discussing the best place to hang them. Throughout the day, many of the people Anna had met the night before came to the gallery to see the new paintings. In the afternoon they were sitting in the back having a cup of tea when the bell announced someone's entry. Looking up Anna saw the lady from the shop where she had bought the statue of the gnome. The lady walked straight to the back where she gave Lilith a hug, and Lilith turned to Anna and introduced the lady as her mother, Lynette.

They talked for a while and Lynette said that she had stopped to find out if Lilith needed any help with the party on Saturday. Lilith had planned a party as a way to introduce Anna to her friends, but they had been so busy with the paintings all morning that she had not thought to tell Anna about it yet. She explained that it would be a very casual gathering and that Anna could go to her room whenever she wanted. Anna was very excited about being with Lilith's friends and assured her she would not want to get away. Lynette made a list of things to bring to the party, kissed Lilith goodbye and told Anna she was happy to have seen her again.

Lilith and Anna had just gotten the last of the paintings in place when a very handsome man, who looked to be about Lilith's age, entered the gallery. He walked back to where they were standing and took Lilith in his arms and kissed her deeply. They both laughed when they saw the look on Anna's face and Lilith introduced the man as Daniel, an art dealer and a dear friend. They talked as he walked around the gallery and looked at the paintings. He paused for a long time in front of Anna's paintings and finally chose six of hers and one other. When Lilith told him that Anna was the artist who had painted the pictures, he asked her where she got such wonderful ideas and remarked that she certainly had a wonderful imagination. Anna looked at Lilith who shook her head slightly, and she knew that this was not someone she could discuss this with. Anna thanked him for the compliments and walked to the back of the gallery to give them privacy to say goodbye.

After Daniel left, Lilith told Anna that she had arranged for a friend to take care of the gallery for her on Friday and Saturday, so that they could have time together. She then walked to the desk and came back with a check, which she handed to Anna and said she would take her to the bank tomorrow to deposit it. When Anna looked at the check, she protested that it was far too much. Lilith told her that her paintings were selling for very high prices, and she was making a good commission on them, so Anna should not feel bad about taking the money. Lilith said her income had doubled since she started selling Anna's work, and she expected it to continue to increase as Anna became better known.

Once again they stopped at the restaurant on the way home and had a wonderful light meal of chicken salad with nuts and fruit mixed in. Anna made a mental note of the ingredients so that she could try this when she got back home because it was so delicious. When they arrived home, Lilith suggested they get their baths and then talk until they were ready to go to bed. She walked over the bridge with Anna and opening the closet pulled out what she called a caftan of rich, pastel colors in a random pattern and told Anna she could put this on after her bath. Anna ran water in the tub, sprinkled some of the lavender oil in it and stepped in enjoying the heady scent. After she had bathed, she slipped the caftan over her head luxuriating in the caress of the soft fabric against her damp, clean skin. She ran a comb through her hair and walked across the little bridge to the living room where the door stood open and soft music could be heard in the background. There were scented candles burning around the room that mixed with the fragrance of the flowers. Lilith came out wearing a caftan herself and explained to Anna that she often wore these when she was at home. As they talked, Anna asked Lilith about some of the things she had heard discussed that she did not understand and told her she had always been told these things were evil. Lilith explained that all people were working toward advancement and were at different levels. Anna then asked Lilith about her life as a child and was fascinated as Lilith talked about growing up with Lynette. She told Anna that she had been married to Daniel, and they loved each other very much, but their beliefs were too different for them to be able to live together. She explained that she just could not conform to the standard idea of what a wife should be and found that she was really much happier living alone. She smiled as she admitted, however, that Daniel sometimes stayed overnight, and she enjoyed the lovemaking very much. That night as Anna lay in bed remembering the way that Lilith and Daniel had kissed, she wondered if she would ever know what that was like.

Chapter 13

The following morning after a leisurely breakfast and a few cups of tea Lilith and Anna retired to their rooms to dress for the day. Lilith had told Anna this was her day, and they could do whatever she wanted. Anna said the only thing she could think of was to go to the bank, shop for some painting supplies and perhaps visit Lynette's shop again. They stopped at the bank first, where Anna deposited her check, and then drove to Lynette's shop, as Lilith had told her there was also a shop that sold painting supplies just around the corner.

Lynette was busy with a customer when they entered, so they just looked around while Lilith explained things that Anna did not understand and pointed out a couple of books she thought Anna would find interesting. When Lynette had finished with her customer, she came over and gave them both a hug. Since there was no one else in the shop, they went to the back where Lynette offered them tea or hot chocolate. They both chose hot chocolate as they stated they had already had too much tea.

They talked for a while about mutual friends of Lynette and Lilith, and Anna was caught off guard when Lynette suddenly asked if she had considered painting as a way of earning a living instead of working as a maid. Anna told them she had never even thought of this, and Lynette pointed out how much more time she would have to paint and maybe even be able to travel and see different things to get ideas. When they had finished their hot chocolate, Anna purchased one of the books Lilith had suggested, and they said goodbye.

As they approached the shop Lilith had told her about, they passed a realtor and stopped to look in the window as Anna remarked she was curious about what a house would cost. As they stood looking in the window and talking about owning a home, Anna found herself becoming very excited about the idea of having her own place someday. They were still talking about houses when they entered the art supply shop.

The place where Anna had always bought her supplies sold general merchandise, but this shop sold only art supplies, and she was stunned at the variety of things available. As they looked around, Lilith answered questions and made a couple of observations, but she did not interfere with Anna's choices. She had suggested Anna keep quite a bit of money out when they went to the bank in case she saw something she liked, and they left the store loaded down with painting supplies.

By this time they were getting quite hungry. They decided to buy some food and have a picnic in the country and purchased fruits, cheeses, fruit juices, cold cuts, crackers, cups, plates and napkins, which Anna insisted on paying for as Lilith had paid for everything to this point. Lilith drove to where there was a nice lake with swans and picnic tables, and they spread their feast. As they ate, Anna noticed a family of little people under a bush beside the table, and she put some food broken into very small pieces on a napkin and placed it under the bush. In a short while, more little people had gathered to share in the feast, and Anna placed more food under the bush. Lilith was unable to see the little people, but she knew what was going on and for the first time she saw the unselfish caring that was a part of Anna and understood what it was that made it possible for Anna to see things that others could not.

Anna asked if Lilith would mind her doing some painting and was urged to do so. They both went to the car and brought back the supplies. After several unsuccessful attempts at working with the new paints, Anna began to paint. Lilith sat watching and realized that Anna actually entered that world when she worked. Several children brought a ball and began to play close by, and Anna was not even aware of their presence. No wonder her paintings are so special, thought Lilith, she is actually there. She also understood why Tom had resented her painting so much and wondered if Anna would ever find anyone who would be able to accept this detachment from the mundane world.

Lilith was also astonished at the speed with which Anna painted, which explained how she did so many paintings when she worked so much. After about three hours, the painting was finished and Anna suddenly turned to look at Lilith apologizing for not talking to her. Lilith told her not to worry because it had been a pleasure to watch her work, and she had enjoyed it very much. They sat for a while nibbling on the food that was left, and Anna cut more into small pieces and placed it under the bush. Anna had painted the lake with the swans and on the bank and a village of little people under a spreading bush. There was a large, gnarled tree just back from the lake and as Lilith looked closer she saw a face in the tree and realized that Anna had contacted another part of the unseen world when she sat with her back against the tree. Lilith was able to sense these things, but she envied Anna the ability to see them.

When they reached the house, Lilith asked Anna if she liked to swim. Anna answered that she did not swim well but she really liked the water, so Lilith found a suit that she thought would fit, and they went to their rooms to change. When Anna came back into the courtyard, Lilith had lit the small lights and it looked like a dream world. There was music playing softly in the background and the air was filled with the fragrance of all the flowers. They slid into the water and swam slowly the length of the pool. Anna had not thought about how clever this pool was but unlike most it was long and narrow, which was very good for swimming without wasting water and much more esthetically appealing. When she remarked on this, Lilith thanked her and told her it had been her idea. She said she had argued with the builder for a long time because he did not want to build it this way. She pointed out that it was also much easier to care for with it being only seven feet wide.

After the swim, they bathed, donned the caftans and met back in the main room where they each stretched out on a sofa and read for a while. Lilith suggested a light snack before bed, and they raided the kitchen for leftovers. As they ate, Anna told Lilith that she had never enjoyed anything so much as being here and how soothing and perfect her home was. Lilith thanked her and said this was her refuge from the sometimes ugly and callous world. They hugged as they said goodnight and went to their beds. Anna dreamed of being in a world of magic with tall castles of crystal in all the colors of the rainbow.

She awoke the next morning and picked up a sketchpad as she went to sit in the courtyard. The air was heavy with fog that gave everything a feeling of mystery, and she sketched quickly to catch the magic before the fog lifted. Lilith saw that she was busy and went to start breakfast without disturbing her. As the sun spilled into the courtyard and chased away the fog, Anna looked around and saw Lilith standing in the doorway and once again apologized for being so selfishly preoccupied. Lilith smiled, gave her a hug as she brushed aside her apology and asked to see the sketch. Anna had never shown her any sketches, and she was amazed at the simplistic beauty of this. She had managed to capture the magic with only a pencil and paper and somehow it seemed more pure and special than the paintings. She asked if Anna had other sketches and was told that she had many.

After breakfast they both worked cleaning the house and preparing for the party that afternoon. Lilith told Anna that the guests would begin arriving around three that afternoon and the party would last until around eight or nine that evening. She also said she had hired a caterer so that they could enjoy the party without having to work.

At one in the afternoon Lilith went to her room and returned with a long, flowing hostess gown and handed it to Anna. She said this would be the way most people were dressed and she wanted Anna to feel relaxed and enjoy herself, and they retired to their rooms to get ready. Since they had plenty of time, Anna soaked in the scented water and let her mind drift away.

She saw herself standing facing a fork in the road trying to decide which way to go. She could not see what lay down either road, but she felt that her decision was crucial. She was brought back to the present by cooling water and finished bathing, washed her hair and dried herself on the thick, fluffy towel. As the gown slipped over her head, Anna felt transformed. She had never worn anything so luxurious, and it made her feel more confident.

The first guests to arrive were Lynette and almost immediately afterward Daniel, and once again Daniel and Lilith kissed with a passion that almost made Anna blush. They got drinks and settled themselves on the sofas. Lilith had left Anna's sketch on a table in the corner, and Daniel went over to take a closer look at it. Lilith told him that Anna had other sketches, but she had not seen them and had been unaware how skilled she was in this medium. Anna noticed that they did not discuss the things they normally did and realized that Daniel did not believe as Lilith and Lynette did about things. Other guests soon began arriving and at five in the evening Lilith announced the food was ready.

Everything was served buffet style and very casual. There was soft music playing, candles were burning inside and out with dim lights, and all of the sliding doors were open, so the courtyard and house were combined to form a large space where people moved from one small group to another. Lilith asked for everyone's attention and said a prayer of thanksgiving for the food and company, and everyone filled their plates and found a place to eat.

After they had eaten, Lilith took Anna around and introduced her to everyone, and Anna noticed that there were many more women than men. She recognized many that she had met at the restaurant but had forgotten the names because she had met so many at one time. She was drawn into one group after another and found the conversations very interesting but confusing, and she found that she wanted to know about everything. She asked many questions and everyone seemed pleased to explain what they were talking about. Around seven in the evening some of the guests began leaving and Lilith asked Anna to join her in saying goodbye.

When things had quieted down, Anna noticed that the dozen or so people who remained were mostly those she had met before. They all ended up in the living room sitting on the sofas or the floor in a circle, and one of the men suggested they do a meditation. He told them to just get comfortable and close their eyes, and imagine themselves on a beach far from the modern world. As he talked, Anna felt herself go into the scene even though she had never been to a beach. She felt the sand between her toes, smelled the ocean and heard the waves breaking and the call of the seagulls.

When the meditation was over, she was reluctant to leave that wonderful place, and she asked Lilith how she could have felt as though she were there when she had never left this room. Everyone joined in a discussion about time and space and whether they had actually been on the beach, and they told her that it was possible to be in two places at one time. They talked quietly for about an hour, and then the remainder of the guests rose to leave. Anna and Lilith stood at the doorway as the guests left, and each of them kissed Anna on the cheek and welcomed her to their group. After the last of the guests had left, Lilith and Anna took a cup of tea to the courtyard while the caterers cleaned up, and Lilith asked if she would like to go to her church the next day. Anna smiled and said she had hoped to be invited.

Anna had brought one of her nice dresses in case they went to church, but the next morning, Lilith brought out a very soft, flowing dress of pale lavender and asked if Anna would like to wear it. She had noticed that most of Lilith's friends wore clothing like this and was grateful for the chance to wear such beautiful things, so she thanked Lilith and took the dress to her room to get ready.

She had expected the church to be special and was very surprised to see that it was just a store front in a run down area of town. Inside everything was very simple with just padded straight-backed chairs and an unpretentious podium. There was incense burning and soft music playing, and everyone greeted with a hug and stood talking quietly. When it was time for the service, one of the women Anna had met asked everyone to stand and join in saying The Great Invocation. As they read from the sheets that had been placed on each seat, she felt something deep within her resonate to the words and thought this was certainly more beautiful than any prayer she had ever heard before.

The woman next read the announcements of upcoming events and classes that were being taught at the church, and it all sounded so interesting that Anna longed to be able to join in. The pastor then approached the podium and spoke about the purpose of life and how we get back what we give out to others. Anna sat transfixed as she heard that there was a reason for everyone to be here and that when the time came to leave this earth we would all rejoin those who had gone before and work on ways to improve ourselves in preparation for the next time.

There was no talk of heaven or hell except what we choose for ourselves as a way of atoning for past mistakes or to pay a debt to someone we had wronged. The pastor pointed out that sometimes people we pity may have chosen a very hard life either to repay a karmic debt or as an example to others because they are very advanced as many believe was the case with Jesus. She also talked about those who do great harm to others and said that we should feel pity for them because of what they will have to endure to make up for this.

When the service ended, Anna found herself longing to know more and to be able to be a part of this group. Money was collected, and they stood for the Benediction. These words also struck a cord deep within Anna, and she asked Lilith if it would be all right for her to take the paper that contained The Great Invocation and Benediction and was told they would be pleased for her to. Everyone gathered in another room where snacks were laid out and coffee and tea were available. They discussed the different points of the service and Anna was able to ask questions, which everyone seemed happy about.

It was soon time to go back to Lilith's, so that she could drive Anna home, and Anna said a reluctant goodbye to everyone as she turned to leave with tears in her eyes. She was very quiet on the drive and Lilith did not ask any questions as she could see that Anna was being torn by her desire to stay and her duty to go. Back at the house, they packed everything and then sat in the courtyard for one last cup of tea. Anna attempted to tell Lilith how much being here had meant to her, but she broke down and could not talk. Lilith put her arms around Anna's shoulders and told her that when the time was right she would be a part of this life, and in the meantime she was welcome to visit whenever she had the opportunity. On the drive, they talked about the things Anna had heard discussed that she did not understand and the people she had met.

Chapter 14

The car had barely stopped when Mr. and Mrs. Connors came to meet them and Mrs. Connors gave Anna a big hug and told her how much they had missed her. They both said hello to Lilith, and Mr. Connors helped carry Anna's bags in. Mrs. Connors had a snack laid out with fresh, hot bread, and Lilith accepted an invitation to join them. Anna told them about her visit with the family and about meeting Lilith's mother and the party, being very careful of course not to mention the details that she knew they would disapprove of. When Lilith asked about Anna's sketches, Anna went to her room and returned with several sketchpads, which Lilith spent some time looking at. She said these were wonderful, and she was sure they would sell very well and asked if she could take them with her.

Anna walked out with Lilith, and as the car pulled away, she felt suddenly very lonely. She decided she would like to walk down to the stream behind the house and returned to the kitchen to ask if there was anything she could help with and to let the Connors know where she would be. Mrs. Connors sensed that there was something different about Anna, and she wondered if they were going to be losing her. This thought made her sad because Anna had become almost like a daughter and she enjoyed her company.

For once Anna had not brought anything to paint or draw with, and she sat beside the stream lost in thought going over the last few days that had seemed almost like magic. She heard a noise and turned to see the gnome sitting beside her. She told him about her visit with Lilith and how much she had wanted to stay, and he smiled as he said, "When the time is right." Anna was surprised and told him that was the same thing Lilith had said, and he just smiled again. She felt as if there was some great secret that everyone knew except her, and she wanted very much to be a part of whatever it was. She suddenly realized that she was quite tired and rose to return to the house after saying goodnight to the gnome.

The Burkes were returning on Wednesday, and there wasn't a lot to do, so Anna was able to spend most afternoons and each evening painting and sketching. She returned to the special glade and found that she saw things differently than before. She was seeing a light glowing around everything that seemed to change colors and pulse. Her paintings took on even more intensity and a mystical quality because of the light. She was happy to be back in a way, but she felt a longing for the softness that she had discovered at Lilith's. She now burned candles in her room and enjoyed the sound of a small wind chime she had bought and hung in her window as it tinkled softly in the breeze.

On Wednesday afternoon the Burkes returned, and Anna and Mrs. Connors were busy preparing meals while Mr. Connors carried bags and laid fires, and life returned to normal. As the days passed, Anna became more settled in her life here, and Mrs. Connors was very relieved that she seemed to be back to herself. Anna still painted whenever she could, and she had developed different techniques using the new supplies she had bought. She found that she was also doing more watercolors again and that she was much better with them than before.

That Sunday she went to church and was struck by the difference in the actions of people from those she had met at Lilith's church as they made unkind comments about others and only talked to those they felt were worthy. She noticed a family standing to the side that she had not seen before and went over to speak to them. Their clothes were very worn but clean, and they seemed uncomfortable standing all by themselves. Anna introduced herself and asked if they lived nearby. The woman introduced them all and said they has just moved onto a farm down the road and were going to be farming it for the owner. She said they were Nora and Hank Tindall, and their two girls were Alice and Jeannie, and they had a son named Robert who had stayed home today because he was just getting over a slight cold. Anna walked into the church with the Tindalls and sat with them through the service.

As they left the church Mr. and Mrs. Connors came over and Anna introduced them. Tom also came over and was introduced and asked Anna about her vacation. She talked about her visit with her family and Lilith, and he asked if she was coming to the dance the next week. Anna answered that she was and then invited Alice and Jeannie who seemed excited by the prospect, but she noticed that Mrs. Tindall didn't seem too happy about it.

That afternoon Anna decided to walk over and visit the Tindalls, and Mrs. Connors gave her part of a cake from the night before to take to them. She changed clothes and gathered her painting supplies before starting out across the open meadow. She was familiar with the area now and knew that it would be much shorter than going by the road, and she always preferred the open country and solitude anyway. She waved as she passed homes along the way and suddenly felt better than she had since returning. It took almost an hour to walk to the farm, but she enjoyed it and was almost disappointed to find that she had arrived. The family was sitting on the porch as she approached and offered the cake that Mrs. Connors had sent.

Mrs. Tindall offered her a cool glass of lemonade, which Anna accepted gratefully, and Mr. Tindall insisted she sit in the rocking chair as he went to sit on the steps. The girls asked about her bag, and Anna explained that she liked to paint and always took these things with her. While she was showing them the different paints and things, a young man came around the house, and Mrs. Tindall said this was their son Robert.

Anna looked up, and her breath caught in her throat as she looked into deep blue eyes that seemed to see into her very soul. His shirt was open, and his muscles rippled under deeply tanned skin that seemed to glow with a light misting of perspiration. He reached out and took her hand, and she felt a shock run up her arm. He apologized as he quickly buttoned his shirt and said he had been working in the barn and didn't realize they had company. He appeared to be slightly older than her, but he acted much older as he got a glass of lemonade and sat on the steps beside his father, and they began to talk about the farm and what would be needed to get it going. He told his father the equipment was in very poor condition, but he should be able to get it running.

The girls asked Anna about the dance, and Mrs. Tindall interrupted saying they didn't have anything to wear, but Anna assured her that it was very informal and no one dressed up, which made the girls very happy. She mentioned some of the other activities that they might be interested in, and Robert spoke up and said they were all going to be too busy to do a lot of playing because it would take all of them to get this place running. After a few minutes, Anna excused herself and said she had better be on her way. She thanked Mrs. Tindall for the lemonade and said she looked forward to seeing them all again.

On the way home, she stopped under a large oak tree and took out her sketchpad and began sketching only to realize later that she had included Robert in the scenery. Anna was awash in emotions that she had never experienced before, and as she looked at the sketch, she thought that perhaps the stories of love were true after all. When she entered the kitchen Mrs. Connors noticed she had more color in her cheeks and asked if she had overtired herself. Anna assured her she hadn't and went to put her things away before dinner. The following day Mrs. Connors went to Anna's room looking for her and saw the sketch of Robert. As she looked at it, she was sure she understood the reason for Anna's increased color and hoped that she didn't end up hurt.

Saturday evening she hurried to the dance hoping against hope that Robert would be there with Alice and Jeannie, but she saw the girls standing outside alone and felt let down. As she walked toward the girls, she passed a group of the girls from the more affluent families in the area and overheard them making fun of the way Alice and Jeannie were dressed. These girls had always irritated Anna with their snobbish attitude, and before she knew what she was doing she had walked over up to their group and looking them each in the eye told them that a ragged, ugly soul was much worse than a ragged, ugly dress. The girls turned red faced with embarrassment and turned to go inside without another word. She then went to where Alice and Jeannie were standing and taking them each by an arm walked them inside and introduced them to all of her friends. They never knew what had happened because they had been too far away to hear, and they had a wonderful time.

Chapter 15

Anna had hoped that Robert would be with the family at church on Sunday, but once again she was disappointed. After church, Mrs. Tindall thanked her for being so nice to the girls and told her they had really enjoyed themselves. She talked to the family and Tom and some of the other young people for a while and then started back to the house to get her paints and go for a walk. Since she had the rest of the day off, she decided to go to the special glade. When she got there, she set everything up and was soon lost in painting the wonderland that presented itself to her, and as usual, her spirits lifted with joy as she entered this world. The sun was low in the sky when she had finished and returned fully to the physical world and climbed the rise to start for home. As she turned for a last look, she saw the angel and her parents standing by the pool smiling at her and heard the small voice whisper, "We are with you always."

Her days settled once again into the usual routine of work and painting whenever the opportunity arose, but now she felt a restlessness that she had not felt before. She found herself walking in the direction of the Tindall's farm whenever she had enough time and found a mill with a small dam that she liked to paint. One afternoon the Burkes informed Mrs. Connors that they would be out for dinner, and since Anna had finished her work by three in the afternoon she had the remainder of the day off. She gathered her painting supplies and went to the mill. Ever since her visit with Lilith, she had been experimenting with new colors and techniques, and she was lost in this when she suddenly felt the urge to turn around and saw Robert standing looking dejectedly out across the fields toward their farm. He had not seen her because she was half hidden behind a bush, and she rose and started toward him. He whirled around as she drew near and the look on his face tore at her heart. She asked if anything was wrong at home, and he answered that everything was wrong. He said the equipment was all broken down, and the harder he tried the more went wrong. He said he had missed the best part of the growing season, and if he didn't get crops in soon it would be too late for anything, and he didn't know what the family would do because they had no money and were almost out of food except for what they got from the small vegetable garden his mother and the girls had planted.

As he talked, Anna sensed his desperation and the heavy burden he carried and wanted more than anything to comfort him. She could think of nothing to say but told him she wished she could help, and he really looked at her for the first time. He apologized and was obviously embarrassed about losing control. To change the subject, she explained that she had been painting, and he walked over to look at the painting she had been working on. He stood looking at the picture for quite a while and complimented her on her ability to capture the true essence and spirit of the place. She could have stayed there by his side forever, but he said he had to get back to work and turned to leave. After he left, she tried to paint but was unable to concentrate for thinking about the plight of his family.

She suddenly had an idea and hurriedly packed her supplies and headed for Tom's house. Tom saw her approaching and went to meet her concerned that something was wrong. They sat on an old log, and Anna told him about her meeting with Robert, and Tom said he was glad she had come to him because he was sure he could get the neighbors together to help them out. By this time it was quite late, and he insisted on saddling his horse and taking her home. He helped her in the saddle and then mounted behind. Anna felt safe and warm with his arms around her and was unaware of the turmoil he felt. He wanted more than anything to take her in his arms and kiss her with all the passion that was pulsing through him, and it took a supreme effort to talk calmly about ordinary things while he felt the warmth of her body against his chest and smelled the scent of her hair as it blew against his cheek. When they reached the Burkes home, he was both relieved and reluctant to dismount and help her from the horse. Anna was unaware of his feelings as Tom stood with his hands clinched to keep from grabbing her when she kissed him on the cheek and said goodnight. As he rode home in the gathering darkness, he wondered if he would ever get over his love for her.

The following day, Mr. Connors told them that Tom was getting all of the neighbors together to help the new family, and Anna felt very relieved. That Sunday when they approached church, she noticed that Robert was standing with the rest of the family and felt her heart leap with joy at the sight of him. She walked over, and the girls began telling her how everyone had come over and helped plow and plant the fields and the women had brought food for everyone and a lot of it was left over. The church bells rang, and as they turned to enter the church, Robert touched her arm and led her to sit with his family. She had no idea what was said in church that day because she was so acutely aware of his nearness, and her heart beat rapidly at the slightest touch of his arm against hers. As they left the church many people came over to say hello to the Tindalls and to shake Mr. Tindall's and Robert's hands, and the women talked to Mrs. Tindall and the girls as Anna walked over to where Mr. and Mrs. Connors were talking to some of their friends. As Anna approached, Mrs. Connors again saw the color in her cheeks and knew that she was hopelessly in love with this very handsome young man. She noticed that he had also attracted the attention of all the other young ladies, and she said a silent prayer that Anna would not be badly hurt.

As they turned to start home, Robert approached and asked if he could talk to Anna for a moment and said he would walk her home. They walked slowly in silence for a while until they were away from everyone else, and then he told her that he knew she was responsible for the help they had gotten and didn't know how he would ever be able to thank her. She answered that she had not done anything but was very happy that things were better for his family. She mentioned her surprise at seeing him at church, and he said he had come because he wanted to thank her.

They had cut across open country to save time, and as they came to a shady spot under a tree Robert took her arm and turned her to face him. She looked into his eyes, and her heart soared as he took her in his arms and kissed her deeply. This was nothing like any kisses she had ever gotten, and it stirred feelings she had never felt before. They walked the rest of the way in silence with him holding her hand, and she felt as though her feet weren't even touching the ground.

After he left, Anna ate a quick lunch and gathered her painting supplies and went to the glade. It took quite a while for her emotions to settle down, but she was soon lost in her painting, and the peace of the place settled over her. She rose to leave as the sun got low and as usual, she turned to take a last look at the top of the rise. The scene was one of magic with fairies flying among the balls of light that floated through the air, the angel standing by the pool and little people and elves dancing under the willow.

The following day, Anna told Mrs. Connors how she had met Robert by accident and then told Tom about the family being in trouble, and that Robert had walked her home because he had wanted to thank her. Although Mrs. Connors thought there was probably a lot more to it than that, she didn't say anything. The following Sunday Anna looked expectantly for

Robert, but he never came back to church, and as the weeks passed, she resigned herself to not seeing him again. A couple of times she did take some food that Mrs. Connors gave her for his family, but she seldom saw him, and he was always very casual when she did.

It was full summer now, and Jason came home from college for a full month. Several of his friends came to stay for a few days during this time, so there was a lot more work to be done. Anna seldom had time to do any painting except for Sundays and those rare occasions when the Burkes all went out for dinner. She did find time most evenings to do some sketching beside the stream, but she was too tired to walk any farther. Even though the days were longer, she found herself falling into bed most nights as soon as the sun went down.

She began packing a light lunch and taking her painting supplies with her on Sundays to save the time of having to come back to get them. This gave her the opportunity to wander farther away, and she discovered a very wonderful spot in a heavily wooded area. This was quite a distance from home, so she had to be careful to leave before dark as it was almost a two-hour walk home. There was an old cabin nestled in a small clearing among the trees with wild roses climbing up the porch and running across the roof. She returned here every Sunday for weeks, and there was never anyone around, but she stayed outside and painted. The trees were very tall and thick, so it always seemed like twilight. The balls of light darted among the trees as though playing hide and seek. The forest floor was filled with gnomes, fairies and elementals of all types. She tried different mediums but was unable to capture the haunting quality of the scene until one day she finally got the right mixture of colors. When she finished this painting, she knew that it was one of the best she had ever done. She had been reluctant to stop and painted later than usual, so it was fully dark when she arrived home, and she was very tired. Mrs. Connors asked if she was all right, and she answered that she was just very tired and hungry. She explained that she had not wanted to quit until she finished the painting, and when she showed it to Mr. and Mrs. Connors they were speechless at the beauty of the scene that shimmered with a silvery glow. Mrs. Connors fixed her a plate of food while she cleaned up, and she was barely able to stay awake long enough to eat.

The following morning Mrs. Burke told them that she was having a small dinner party on Thursday, and she and Mrs. Connors sat down to discuss the menu. Anna knew that Jason was leaving at the end of the week and things would be easier then, but before he left all of his laundry had to be finished in addition to getting ready for the party. Because of the number of guests, the house had been thoroughly cleaned, so it was merely a matter of keeping up with everything. Anna had no time that week to do anything except work and by the time Saturday evening came she was glad to just sit beside the stream and relax. Jason had left that afternoon, and she had cleaned his room before dinner, so there was nothing else to worry about until Monday. As she sat by the stream, the gnome came and sat beside her. She told him about Robert and how much she wanted to be with him. The gnome just listened and when she had finished talking he told her that everything was as it should be, and she just had to let things work out the way they were meant to be.

The next day none of the Tindalls were at church, and Anna decided to walk over and make sure there was nothing wrong. As she neared the house, she heard someone in the house shouting obscenities and loud thumping sounds. She hesitated unsure what to do and saw Robert walking quickly toward her. When he reached her side, he took her arm and led her away across the fields to the mill without saying a word. When they reached the mill, he sat on the grass, and she sat beside him. He sat looking across at the mill with a look of anger on his face, and when he finally turned to look at her, she sensed that he was also very ashamed. He told her that he had hoped the move here would make a change in his father, but he just could not stay away from liquor, and when he drank he became very mean. She began to understand why Robert worked so hard and was the one that was responsible for everything, as he talked about having to take care of his mother and sisters because his father couldn't. He told her that his mother's family had left them a farm of their own when he was very young, but they had lost everything because his father had done no work and mortgaged the farm to get money for liquor.

Anna reached out and pulled his head into her lap and sat stroking his hair while he talked about the dreams he had of someday owning his own place and being able to hold his head up with pride. She felt the pain in his words and longed to be able to do something to ease it. After about an hour, Robert looked up and putting his hands behind her head drew her lips to his in a long, searching kiss. He stood up slowly and pulled her to her feet as he took her in his arms and pressed her body to his. She felt as though fire were running through her veins and tried briefly to pull away before giving into the passion that raged between them. Suddenly Robert stepped back and turned away breathing deeply. She stood motionless waiting for him to say something, but he just stayed with his back to her until she finally reached out tentatively to touch him on his shoulder and ask if she had done something wrong. Robert turned then and gently put his arm around her shoulder and told her she had done nothing wrong, but he had to stop what they were doing before he lost control and did something they would both regret.

They sat back down on the grass, and he thanked her for always seeming to be there when he needed someone. She asked how things were going with the farm, and he said that thanks to her and the neighbors everything was good. The weather had been perfect, and it looked like they would have a very good crop, and there would be enough money to buy some equipment so that next year would be easier. As he talked about farming, his face lost the look of anger and hurt, and he forgot about the family problems. He talked about the smell of fresh turned soil and how everything smelled clean and fresh after a rain. He told her he often slept in the barn during the summer and especially when it was raining, so that he could feel a part of the earth and the elements.

She talked about the small village where she had lived until her mother died and about how she felt when she was painting, but was careful not to mention the things she saw. The sun had sunk low on the horizon when they finally stood to go their separate ways. He took her in his arms once again and kissed her very gently before stepping away from her with a smile. Anna gathered her painting supplies and started home. She looked back before walking out of sight and saw Robert standing watching her. They waved, and he turned to make his way home.

The next week the work returned to normal with Jason gone and the dinner party behind them, and Anna was able to spend time painting. On Sundays she often went to the mill to paint and Robert would join her there. Their kisses grew more passionate each time they met, and she longed for more, but he always pushed her away before things got out of hand. For the first time, she was able to paint with someone else with her. He would sit while she painted and talk about his dreams of a farm, and she did several paintings of him lying on the grass with the mill in the background.

Chapter 16

One Saturday afternoon, a couple of weeks after Jason returned to college, Anna saw Lilith's car pull up beside the kitchen door. She ran out and threw her arms around Lilith before she had time to even close the car door. They talked for a while about what had been going on. Anna told her that she had not done as much painting because of the added workload and explained that she had done mostly sketches. Lilith told her that the sketches had sold very well and had brought more that she expected, so she had a good-sized check for her. She handed the check to Anna explaining that it also included most of the paintings as well. This check was more than what she already had in the bank, and Anna could hardly believe her eyes. They entered the kitchen and Mrs. Burke, who had seen the car drive up, greeted Lilith and invited her to join her and Mr. Burke for dinner. Lilith declined saying that she had dinner plans in town and had just come to bring Anna a check and to see if she had more paintings.

Anna made several trips to her room to get paintings and sketches while Mrs. Burke and Lilith talked about what a wonderful artist Anna was as they looked through them. When Lilith saw the paintings of Robert, she knew that Anna finally had the answers to her questions about love. There were quite a few paintings of the cabin in the woods that she had done before she achieved the effect she wanted, and Lilith complimented her on these, but when she brought the last picture she had done of it, Mrs. Burke said she had never seen anything so beautiful. Lilith told her it was even better than the figure at the waterfall, and Anna lined the pictures up to show how she had experimented until she got the look she wanted. Looking at this, Mrs. Burke knew that she would soon be without a maid, and she was going to miss Anna as a maid but that she had also grown quite fond of her.

They carried the paintings and sketches out to Lilith's car, and Anna's eyes filled with tears as she said goodbye. She watched as Lilith drove away and then walked down to the stream where she took the check out of her pocket and looked at it. She had never thought much about the money that she was putting in the bank, but now she realized she had a lot of money and could do whatever she wanted to do. The problem was, she had never thought about what she wanted to do and had no idea what that could be. She thought about going to live in town where she could be with Lilith and her friends, but then she would not be able to see Robert. She sat for a long time torn between memories of the time she had spent with Lilith and the way she felt when she was in Robert's arms.

The next day, she skipped church and took her painting supplies to the glade where she had not been for a while hoping to get some insight into what she should do. It was a cloudy day, and she had just gotten everything laid out when a fog formed in the glade giving it a special look. She worked hurriedly to mix her paints to capture the beauty of this scene and continued working for hours until she had finished. Once again, she had captured the silvery look of the cabin in the woods, and Anna knew this was a technique she was to develop more fully. Her back was aching from sitting without support for hours, and she stretched out on the damp grass and closed her eyes to relax before starting home. Suddenly she opened her eyes to find the brilliant being standing beside her, and he once again began communicating without speaking. He told her not to try to make a decision because it would all work out the way that it should be, and she should just enjoy each day and let things happen as they are meant to be. When she reached the rise and turned to look back she felt a peace settle over her.

The next day Mrs. Burke told her she could go with Mr. Connors and have him drop her at the bank. She made her deposit keeping out some cash and then hurried to the shop around the corner where she and Lilith had gone. She purchased her supplies and then stopped in at Lynette's shop to say hello. They talked while Anna looked around. She bought a necklace of different colored stones, which Lynette told her were chakra colors, and then said goodbye as she saw Mr. Connors turn the corner. She had heard the term chakra before but had no idea what it meant.

The rest of the week was fairly easy and she was able to spend some time each day working with the new colors and brushes she had bought. There was a dance Saturday, and she went hoping that perhaps Robert would be there. She had not seen Tom or any of the others for quite a while except at church and she explained that she had worked really hard during the summer while Jason was home. She noticed that Tom was spending his time with a girl who lived on an adjoining farm, and she was relieved to know that he had someone now. She left early claiming fatigue but in fact she found that she no longer had any desire to be there.

She took her painting supplies and lunch with her to church the next morning, but Robert was waiting for her, and she decided to take him to the cabin instead of going to church. When they reached the cabin, they stood for a while breathing in the smell of the forest and then Robert walked over to the cabin and opened the door. It was obvious that no one had been here for a long time, and he opened the windows to let in the breeze. Anna used a broom that was standing in the corner to clear a space on the floor and then took a rug from the floor outside, shook it and spread it on the floor. The twilight glow of the deep forest cast a magic glow on them as they sat there and before they knew what was happening they were lying on the rug in each others arms and it was too late to pull away from the feelings that drove them as they kissed. Shivers of desire flooded her being as he ever so gently introduced her to the wonders that the poets write about.

Afterward, she silenced him with a kiss as he begged for her forgiveness. He said he loved her but had nothing to offer because he could barely provide for his mother and sisters, and that duty had to come first. Anna told him she understood and that she had enough money from her paintings to buy a farm of his own and she would help take care of his family. Robert became very upset and said he could never let a woman take care of him, and he could never marry until he could afford to take care of his wife.

They ate the food Anna had brought then closed the cabin and went outside where she painted until it was time to leave. He sat quietly and watched fascinated as she mixed paints and created a picture on the canvas. He helped pack everything up and carried the bag as they walked back home. When they reached the mill, Robert kissed her gently and Anna told him she was not sorry about what had happened because she loved him. He handed her the bag and stood watching until she reached the curve and then waved and turned toward home.

A few days later, Mrs. Burke told Anna that she could have the afternoon off as they were invited to dinner with friends. Anna gathered her painting bag and headed for the mill hoping to see Robert. Shortly after she arrived, she saw him working in a field quite a distance away and began painting the scene. He worked for quite a while before getting close enough to see her and then came to where she sat in the shade of a large oak tree after going to the stream to wash off in the cool water. They sat for a while just enjoying being together and then rose and walked over behind the hedge where they would be hidden from view. This time, Anna felt no pain only the waves of ectasy that washed over her as they made love. They lay in each other's arms and talked for a long time and then returned to the tree where her paints were laid out. He stretched out with his head in her lap as she worked, and she occasionally reached down to run her hand across his forehead or through his hair. He fell asleep, and she watched the lines of worry leave his face as he smiled slightly in his sleep. She woke him with a kiss when it began to grow dark, and he helped her pack everything and walked her home. When they got within sight of the house they kissed a long, lingering kiss goodbye, and she walked quickly the rest of the way.

Chapter 17

Anna was happier than she had ever been. She lived for the times she was able to be with Robert and tried not to think about what his family situation meant for them. Summer was almost over now and with the days growing shorter, it became more and more difficult for them to be together except on Sunday. Once again, she began sitting by the stream close to the house after dinner and doing quick sketches before dark.

The crops had been good, but Robert was still struggling to provide for the family and get the equipment he would need for the next spring. The neighbors had joined together and helped him get the winter crops in, but he knew that he could not expect them to continue to do this. Anna tried time after time to get him to accept a loan from her to buy the equipment and pay her back when he could, but he refused to let her help at all.

Anna awoke one morning and thought that she must be coming down with something. She got dressed and started to the kitchen to help Mrs. Connors with breakfast, but the moment she opened the door and smelled the food cooking, she ran to the bathroom where she vomited until there was nothing left in her stomach and then got dry heaves. Mrs. Connors came to see about her and told her she should just lie down and take it easy for a while. After about an hour, Anna felt better and was able to do her work without any further trouble.

The following morning the same thing happened and when Anna was finally able to come to the kitchen Mrs. Connors very curtly asked if she was pregnant. Anna suddenly sat down at the table in shock. She had trusted that Robert would know what to do to keep this from happening and had not given any thought to the possibility of becoming pregnant. She worked as though in a daze as her mind raced from one possibility to another, and Mrs. Connors' heart melted as she saw what she was going through. When Anna finished with the housework, Mrs. Connors told her to take the rest of the day off, and she would take care of dinner. Anna thanked her and after gathering her painting bag headed for the glade.

When she reached the glade instead of unpacking she went to sit by the pool in the mist from the waterfall and finally the tears began to flow. After a few minutes, she got a drink of water and then went to sit on the bank and think about her options. She knew that Robert loved her and would insist on marrying her if he knew about the baby, but he had so many burdens already that she could not add to them, and she knew he would not let her help. She thought about what it would be like to live with his family and what it would mean for her painting. She also thought about the life that she had experienced with Lilith and knew there was something important she was to do that she could not turn her back on. She had enough money to live on and was sure that Lilith would help her get a place of her own where she could continue to paint and support herself and the baby while she explored the wonderful world she had begun to glimpse while with Lilith.

As she thought about leaving and never seeing Robert again, deep, wrenching sobs tore at her body, and she curled up on the grass and cried until she fell asleep exhausted. Just before she drifted off to sleep, the angel came over, and she felt it wrap its wings around her in protection and comfort. When she awoke, she knew that she had to face the hardest decision she had ever made, but her resolve was strong. The following Sunday she met Robert by the mill after church and told him that she wanted to take him somewhere special. They walked hand in hand as she led him to her special glade.

As they walked down the slope, Robert remarked what a beautiful, peaceful place this was. They went over and got a drink of the cool water and sat down in the shade of the willow tree. Robert had noticed that she did not have her paints with her and sensed that she had an important reason for bringing him here. Anna moved to stand against him, and they made love slowly savoring the pleasure they gave each other and then lay in each other's arms on the cool, soft carpet of grass.

Anna had decided that she would try one last time to get Robert to accept her help, and she raised herself on one elbow and looked into his eyes as she begged him to let her help build a life for the two of them. Robert said he loved her more than anything in the world, but that he just could not accept her money and still feel like a man. She understood that his pride had suffered because of his family's situation and how important this was to him, but her heart broke as he refused her help.

Anna told him that she had an opportunity to live where she could study and develop her painting skills, and that she was no longer content to be a maid. She said she wanted to devote time to her painting because it would provide a more satisfying and fulfilling life and watched as the light went out of his eyes while she talked. When she stopped talking, he said he had nothing to offer and understood how important her painting was to her. They held each other close until the sun got low and then rose and walked home. When they reached the Burkes' home, Robert kissed her gently and said he would love her forever, and then turned and walked quickly away. Anna began to cry and went to the stream to get her emotions under control before entering the house.

Mr. and Mrs. Connors were sitting at the table having dinner when she came in. She sat down at the end of the table and told them she would be leaving soon and would miss them both very much because they had been like a mother and father to her. That night she wrote a letter to Lilith explaining the situation and asking for her help in making the move. Mr. Connors delivered the note on Friday morning, and Anna told Mrs. Burke that she was going to be leaving soon. Mrs. Burke had been expecting Anna to leave long before now and said she would miss her very much but that Anna was far too talented to work as a maid. Anna was content to let Mrs. Burke assume she was leaving because of her painting. She thanked Mrs. Burke for having been so good to work for and told her she had been very happy here.

On Sunday, she decided to stay home and pack instead of going to church, partially because she was afraid that if she saw Robert she would not be able to go and would end up ruining their lives and that of her unborn child. This was the first time she had thought about the child as a person in its own right, and she put her hands on her stomach in a protective gesture at the wonder of what was happening. When she had finished packing, she took one last walk to the glade and sat for a while knowing that she would probably never come here again. She heard the small voice whisper that everything was going to be fine, and she had made the correct decision. At the top of the rise, she turned for one last look and saw her mother and father standing with the angel and the luminescent being by the waterfall and felt their love reach out and wash over her.

She had stopped to sit by the stream and watch the little people for a while and turned at the sound of a car to see Lilith get out of her car and walk toward her. Lilith gave her a hug and then sat beside her on the grass as they talked. She could see the anguish that Anna felt whenever she mentioned Robert and knew what a difficult decision this was for her, but she agreed that it was probably the best solution. Lilith asked if she was ready to leave and Anna told her that everything was packed, so they walked to the house. When they entered the kitchen, Anna told Mr. and Mrs. Connors that she was leaving with Lilith and then went to tell Mr. and Mrs. Burke. She told them that she had cleaned all the rooms that week, apologized for leaving them on such short notice and thanked them for being so kind to her.

Mr. and Mrs. Connors helped carry her belongings out to Lilith's car and after kissing her on the cheek stood and watched as the car drove out of sight. They had become very fond of her, and Mrs. Connors knew that her job was going to be much harder because Anna had been doing all of the housework and helping with the cooking.

Chapter 18

Lilith gave Anna another check the following morning for a staggering amount. She had always seemed to be able to sell as many paintings and sketches as she could get, and as they ate breakfast Anna asked her how she was able to do this. Lilith explained that Daniel knew quite a few art dealers who traveled around the world and had introduced them to her work. She said she had inquiries constantly now wanting more and more pictures, as her work became better known. Anna almost choked on her tea when Lilith told her what she had gotten for the picture of the cabin. She explained that she was now getting three to four times what she had in the past, especially for the paintings with the new technique of a silvery glow that Anna had been using to lend mystery.

In the days that followed, Anna alternated between excitement and utter despair as she faced the reality of her decision, and they began to look for a home for her. Lilith had arranged for a friend to help out with the gallery in order to allow her time to help Anna. Anna had more than enough money, but she had no idea what she wanted to do and was having trouble making decisions. They tried one realtor after another, but she just did not see anything that interested her. After about a week Anna needed more supplies, and they drove to the art supply store. As they approached the store, Anna looked in the window of the small real estate office next door and saw something that caught her interest. They went inside and got directions to a small house on 30 acres and decided to drive out and look at the property. Anna forgot about supplies in her excitement, and Lilith teased her about finally showing some interest.

It was quite a long distance out in the country, and when they turned onto the road that led to the house it was little more than a trail. The land had been neglected, and the house in the distance looked worse. Lilith wanted to just turn around and leave, but something drew Anna to this place, and she insisted they continue. The house was small and in bad condition, but she had the money to make repairs if the cost of the property wasn't too much. There were porches that ran across the entire front and back of the house, and they stood on the back porch looking across a sloping meadow dotted with large shade trees and a fairly large stream that ran beside the house and through the meadow.

On the way back into town Lilith tried to dissuade Anna from this but soon realized there was perhaps more to this decision than even Anna realized. She told Anna to let her do the talking when they returned to the realtor's office, and when they reached the office she told the realtor the price was unreasonable. She said the house was run down and too small, so it would be a liability, and the grounds were so overgrown it would cost a fortune to ever get them cleaned up. The realtor told them that the property was part of an estate and had been on the market for a long time for the very reasons she mentioned, so the family might be willing to take less. Lilith had him draw up an offer for just over half the asking price and they left. She explained to Anna that they had to start low in order to go up just as the seller started high in order to be able to go down.

They stopped by the art supply shop and then at their favorite restaurant on the way back to Lilith's. By this time, Anna was completely comfortable with Lilith's friends and always enjoyed talking to them and learning new things. After dinner they returned to Lilith's and sat in the courtyard sipping tea as Anna worked on a watercolor of the pool and bridge. She pointed out some elves that lived under the bridge, and Lilith wished that she could see them. They talked about the property, and Lilith told Anna she would have to buy a car and learn to drive if she were going to live so far from civilization. They were to return to the realtor the next day, so they planned her first driving lesson for after that.

Anna lay in the tub until the water grew cold and then snuggled into the bed where she dreamed of the little house and her child playing in the meadow while she sat on the porch and painted. She knew that she was carrying a boy who would have the same blue eyes that his father had and hoped this would help ease some of the pain of losing Robert.

Anna awoke early as usual. The morning sickness was getting better and after a few minutes she went to the courtyard to work on the painting from the night before. It was still dark, and a fog had settled, so she worked on the technique that she had been using to give her paintings that aura of magic and mystery. The picture was finished by the time that Lilith came to get her for breakfast. Lilith looked at the picture and said she barely recognized this as her courtyard. Once again, she envied Anna the ability to see this other world so clearly and to recreate it.

They arrived early at the realtor's office because Anna was so restless. When they entered the office, the realtor introduced them to two middle-aged men who were the owners of the property. They said that they had come this morning to try to work out a reasonable price because the offer was so ridiculously low. After 30 minutes of heated bickering, they finally settled on a price that was about one-third less than they had been asking and arranged to meet the following day to finalize the transaction. Anna could barely contain her joy as she signed the papers and received the paperwork for her new home. Naturally, she asked Lilith if they could drive back out to see it, and use that as her driving lesson. Once they were out of traffic, Lilith pulled over and Anna got behind the wheel. She was very nervous, but soon relaxed since she almost had the road to herself. They laughed hysterically as she attempted to turn onto the narrow trail that led to the house and Lilith remarked she would soon have all the brush cleared away as she went from one side to the other.

They talked about all the work that would need to be done and decided to stop on the way back and try to find someone local to do the work. There was a house just at the end of the lane, so they stopped to inquire about hiring help. An elderly man approached the car as they pulled in the drive and directed them to a house a mile farther along the road they were on. A man in his early thirties came out onto the porch when they stopped at the house, and Lilith introduced Anna and herself and explained their reason for being there. The man told them his name was Brian and invited them to join him on the porch where they could sit and talk. He said he was familiar with the house, and he and Anna talked about what she wanted done to it. He did some figuring on costs as they talked and gave her a rough estimate, which Lilith looked over and approved. Even with the cost of the property, Anna had plenty of money to cover this. Since it was Friday, they arranged for him to start on Monday after agreeing that he would be paid as he finished each segment of the job.

Anna drove until they reached the outskirts of town. They stopped by the bank on the way home to get the money for the house and Lilith suggested they just spend a quiet evening at home. They got their baths and then raided the kitchen while they talked. Anna tried to thank Lilith for all of her help, and Lilith said it was the least she could do for the person who was making her rich. Lilith sensed that Anna needed to talk about Robert in order to get this behind her, so she asked questions and then listened as Anna talked. They then talked about how our lives work to lead us the way that we are supposed to go so long as we allow ourselves to be guided by our inner knowing. Anna had been reading one of Lilith's books about reincarnation, and they talked for a long time about this before finally deciding to get some sleep. While they had been talking, Anna had made a sketch of Lilith, which she gave her as they said goodnight. As Lilith looked at the sketch, she noticed that Anna had picked up and painted her aura and was awed once again by her abilities.

Lilith had suggested that they have a driving lesson each day in order for Anna to be ready to drive when it was time for her to move. The next morning they stopped to finalize the paperwork on the house, did some shopping and ran a few errands before turning toward the open country, so that Anna could practice her driving. She was more focused and did quite well even making a few turns without incident, and Lilith suggested she drive back home. She drove until traffic became heavy and then pulled over for Lilith to drive the rest of the way.

Anna asked if they could stop on the way home for her to buy some clothes like those Lilith and her friends wore, and they went to Lynette's shop where she purchased two dresses of light material that draped softly over her body. One was of a lavender and pink swirled color, and the other was white with flowers of pale blue, lavender and pink. This was Saturday and Lilith's friends were all getting together later, so Anna and Lilith returned to the house to put away their purchases and dress for the evening.

Anna had a wonderful time and told them about her new property and had them in tears from laughing as she and Lilith described her driving lessons. The talk soon turned to metaphysical matters, and the hours flew by as Anna listened to them talk and asked questions when she didn't understand what they meant. One of the women told her that they were starting a short three-day class at church on Sunday to discuss the principles of metaphysics and she was welcome to join them. She said they would be meeting each Sunday at the church after services for a couple of hours. Anna looked at Lilith who quickly said she would be glad to stay until the class was over and take her home. It was late when they arrived home that night, and Daniel's car was parked in the drive, so they said goodnight in the courtyard.

Chapter 19

By Sunday, Anna felt confident enough to drive to church, and Lilith said it was about time for her to take her driving test, and then they could find her a car. They stayed after church for the class, and Anna began to understand a little better some of the things she had heard discussed. It all seemed so simple, but the thing that stood out most was the fact that our lives are exactly what we make of them. She thought how wonderful it would be if everyone lived by these principles instead of blaming someone else whenever something went wrong. On the way home, they talked about what they were going to do the next day. They had arranged to meet Brian at the house the next morning so that he would know exactly what she wanted, and Anna asked if Lilith would mind her staying there to paint for the day.

The next morning they were up early and ate a quick breakfast. Anna packed a light lunch and gathered her painting supplies, and then she drove all the way out to the house. This time when she turned onto the road to the house, she had no problem keeping the car on the narrow trail. Brian was already there taking measurements and making notes, so Lilith slid into the driver's seat and told Anna she would be back to pick her up before dark.

Anna and Brian talked about where she wanted the plumbing, walls, closet, et cetera; and he marked everything out in chalk on the floor. The house was divided from side to side with one large room in front and a small room in back. They agreed that the back room should be divided into a small bathroom and combination kitchen and dining room and the front should be divided into a living room and bedroom with the bedroom being the smaller of the two rooms. Anna stressed that she wanted everything to be very plain and simple and explained that the closet should be open on the front, and she would hang a curtain there. After Brian had all the figures, he left to order what he needed and told her he would be back whenever the building supplies could be delivered.

Anna sat on the back porch and painted the meadow with the stream as the sun rose high overhead. She suddenly realized that she was very hungry and took her lunch to the front porch to eat. The property included 30 acres with more depth than width in relation to the road, and the house was toward one side about two-thirds of the way back from the road. When she had finished eating, Anna decided to explore some and started out by walking down the slight incline to the stream. She found a shallow spot and crossed by going from rock to rock and made a note to talk to Brian about building her a bridge. It was difficult to get through the tangled underbrush, but she discovered that there were wild roses, honeysuckle and many other flowers that she was unfamiliar with. She had turned to go back when she saw what looked like an overgrown orchard and made her way over to it. There were apple, pear, plum and cherry trees, but they had not been cared for, and what fruit there was on the trees was small and damaged by insects. She knew this was on her property because of its proximity to the house, and she decided this would be her first priority when it was time to start work on the grounds.

She made her way back to house and found Brian there unloading some things from his truck, and she mentioned that she would like to have a bridge over the stream. He said he had seen the painting she left on the porch and that if she would just draw a picture of what she wanted, he would figure the cost on it. She packed her things into her painting bag then sat on the back porch and made a sketch of the bridge she wanted and took it to him just as she saw Lilith's car coming up the road. Lilith parked the car and then moved to the passenger side, and Anna slid in behind the wheel feeling very confident. As she drove home, she told Lilith about the orchard she had found on her walk, and they talked about the work she was going to have done on the house.

Anna felt messy from her walk through the brush, so they went straight home and worked together getting dinner after their baths. Lilith suggested that Anna take her driving test the next day and then they would start looking for a car, and she nervously agreed. She felt guilty about taking so much of Lilith's time and would be glad when she could do things on her own. After dinner they sat in comfortable silence in the dim candlelight looking out over the courtyard reading and talking occasionally while soft music played in the background. Anna was very tired from the day and excused herself early to go to bed.

She awoke very early the next morning and sat in the courtyard doing a watercolor of a corner of the courtyard where a family of fairies lived. As she sat there lost in their world, she saw the angel on the bridge. She had wondered if she would ever see the angel again, since she would no longer be going to the glade, and was relieved when she heard the small voice say that this was her angel who would always be with her. She returned to her painting and only looked up when it was finished. Once again, she had captured the magic luminescence of the scene, and Lilith joked that they were going to be very rich very soon if she continued at this rate.

Lilith suggested they go out for breakfast, and they returned to their rooms to dress. She gave Anna another large check before they left and suggested that perhaps Anna should open a checking account, since she was going to have so many expenses coming up, and it was better to write checks for large purchases than to carry a lot of cash. Anna opened the checking account with the check Lilith had given her and also transferred some from the savings account to cover the cost of the remodeling and allow for other expenses. She insisted on treating Lilith to a breakfast feast of eggs, bacon, crepes and a variety of fruits. They lingered over tea to let the food settle and talked about what kind of car to look for and the driving test. She was very nervous when they arrived at the testing office, but she did well and walked out 30 minutes later with her license.

They drove around and looked at cars until Anna saw one that interested her. There were many larger, more expensive cars, but Anna was drawn to a small, well-used car that was quite plain. At first Lilith insisted that she could afford something newer and better, but Anna refused to consider even looking at the others. It suddenly occurred to Lilith that perhaps Anna was responding to an inner source in making her decisions, and she made no further effort to influence her. Lilith did take over when the time came to pay for the car, however, and managed to get it for quite a bit less than was asked. The paperwork seemed to take forever, but the salesman finally handed Anna the keys. As he put the keys in her hand, she was suddenly struck by how much her life had changed in such a short time.

She decided to drive out to the house and see if anything was going on. Lilith was hesitant to let her go so far alone, but she knew by now that Anna could be very stubborn once her mind was made up and just asked her not to be too late because she would worry. Anna reached the house without incident and felt a surge of pride and freedom that she had never experienced before. The plumbing was in and Brian was working on insulation for the walls and floor. She would have loved to stay longer, but she didn't want to worry Lilith and be any more of a burden than she was already. The car was easy to handle, and on the way back to town Anna suddenly realized that she enjoyed driving.

She had written to her Aunt Helen to tell her that she had left her job as a maid and was going to support herself with her painting. Now that she had a car she decided to go visit her aunt the next day. She dreaded telling her about the baby, but since they lived so close it would be impossible to keep this from her. Lilith had suggested that Anna tell Helen she would be traveling, but lying was not an option for Anna. Helen was very happy to see her, and ushered her into the living room. She asked if Lilith had dropped her off and looked at Anna in surprise when she said she had driven her own car. As they talked, Helen realized that Anna was no longer the young girl she had brought here but a confident, mature young woman who knew what she wanted and where she was going.

After they had caught up on what had been happening, Anna told Helen she had something very difficult to tell her. She told her about Robert and his family situation and that she loved him more than she had ever thought possible. She then told her that the primary reason she had made the decision to leave was because she was going to have a baby. She explained that she had tried to help with finances, but he would not let her, and she did not want to give up her painting and bring her child into that environment. Anna could tell that Helen disapproved of her decision and thought she should get married and live the kind of life expected of a "good girl." Anna then told Helen that she had come while the rest of the family was gone so that Helen could decide what to tell them and rose to leave. She kissed Helen on the cheek, walked to the car and waved as she drove away.

Chapter 20

Now that Anna had her car, she was able to go every day to the house, and she spent her time wandering the grounds and painting. She saw little people wherever she went, and she felt very happy and peaceful and was eager to make this her home. After two weeks, the major work was done, and they went through the house and talked about the few final decisions to be made. She had mentioned one day as she talked to Brian that she wanted to have swings on both porches and rocking chairs, and the next day when she arrived he had just finished hanging a swing on the front porch. She thanked him and sat down to enjoy it while he returned to work.

The nights were quite cold now, and Anna knew that she had to have heat, so she asked Brian to go with her to advise her on what to buy. He had told her he could get her wood for the winter, and she decided on a wood-burning stove for the living room and a wood cook stove for the kitchen. The stoves were delivered, and the wood was already stacked neatly outside when she arrived on Thursday, and she told Brian she would like to start moving in as soon as the stoves were installed. He said he would be able to get the one for the living room done that day and the one in kitchen definitely by Friday afternoon.

She left early and stopped by the gallery when she reached town to tell Lilith that she was ready to move and to ask for her help with buying furniture. Lilith closed the gallery, and they spent the rest of the day buying furniture, linens, curtains, cooking utensils and all the odds and ends that were needed to run a house. At first Lilith attempted to argue with Anna as she chose very plain, simple furniture with clean lines, but she soon gave up, as Anna was unshakable in what she wanted. Anna arranged to have the furniture delivered the next day, and then they drove out to the house to leave the things they had bought. Lilith had not been to the house since Anna got her car, and as she looked around she realized that everything Anna had bought was perfect for the house. She also noticed how welcoming and comfortable the house was as they sat in the swing on the front porch, and she had the feeling that this place was destined to be something special.

That night they went to the restaurant where they talked for hours about a wide range of subjects as different people joined the group and then left to be replaced by others. As they sat having their last cup of tea before bed, Anna thanked Lilith for all that she had done and said she hoped someday to be able to repay her. Lilith had begun to realize that Anna, by her unfailing example of faith to act on her inner feelings, had shown her the true meaning of the principles she tried to live by, and she told Anna she had already done much more than she knew.

The following morning, after a quick breakfast, Anna packed her things in the car, kissed Lilith on the cheek and drove away after inviting her to come visit anytime. She gently ran her hand over her stomach as she drove and talked to her child about the wonderful life they were going to have. Her eyes filled with tears, however, as she thought how much better it would be if that life were to include Robert, but she brushed away the tears and reminded herself that whatever happened was always for the best.

On Sunday she drove in for church alone for the first time and realized that she belonged here and was truly a part of this group. After church most of them went to the restaurant for lunch before going their separate ways. Anna asked Lilith to let her repay her hospitality by coming for dinner, and Lilith agreed. She had been really lonely since Anna had left and was happy to have her company again.

When they reached the house, Lilith was amazed at the almost magic quality of the small house. There was still work to be done, but Anna had been doing the painting herself and had painted scattered scenes of the little people around the living room so that Lilith felt as though she were able to finally share Anna's vision. They had a light dinner and then bundled up in heavy quilts and sat in the swing looking at the stars. There were no sounds except those of the night, and Lilith felt a deep peace settle over her. They talked about the meaning of life and the complexity of the overall plan for mankind. It was very late when they finally rose shivering from the cold and Anna invited her to stay for the night and made up a cot in the living room where a warm fire burned in the stove. Anna was up early the next morning and got the fires going while Lilith snuggled under the covers until the room was warm.

During breakfast they looked at some of the paintings Anna had done here at the house, and then loaded them in the car for Lilith to take to the gallery. She noticed that there were many pictures with the round balls of light floating through the air and asked if Anna was aware what these were. When Anna answered that she was not, Lilith explained that they are spirits, and they talked for a while about this. As she drove home, she wondered just how special this young woman was who had wandered into her life and who had such vision.

All of the walking that Anna was doing was very good for her, and she felt wonderful as she worked getting her house in order. She had been in her house for about a month when she felt the flutter as her child moved for the first time. Tears of joy filled her eyes as she gently ran her hands around the stomach that was no longer flat. She reveled in the luxury of being able to paint whenever she wanted and to spend her time surrounded by the elementals that seemed to increase every day. She marveled at the way her life had gone from her being a poor, lonely girl to this point all beginning that day at the little stone cottage.

Chapter 21

It seemed that there was always something else to do, so Brian was often around, and Anna knew that he was aware of her pregnancy. One day he brought his wife with him and introduced them because he was concerned about Anna being alone, though he didn't tell her that was the reason. Sarah was very shy with beautiful reddish-blond hair and skin like porcelain, and for the first time Anna felt compelled to paint a portrait. She asked Sarah to sit for her, and Brian told her to go ahead while he got to work. Anna began painting and talking as she worked, and she and Sarah were soon laughing as they shared stories from their lives. Sarah had no real friends other than those at church, and she had been very lonely for someone her own age to spend time with.

Even though Anna had never really done a portrait, it was soon finished and Sarah came over to look at it. Anna had captured the quality of her skin that reflected the light from the window and the hair that seemed to have a life of its own as it cascaded over her shoulders in wild abandonment. Sarah blushed as she looked at the lovely, sensual woman in the painting and asked Anna about the pink glow that seemed to surround her. Anna explained that she often saw a glow around people but didn't really understand what it was. She knew from talking to people at church that this is the aura, but she was reluctant to discuss this with Sarah yet.

When Brian had finished with his work, he came over to see the painting for himself and was amazed as he saw that Anna had captured the sensuality of Sarah as few had ever seen her. As they left, Anna insisted on giving them the painting but asked Sarah to come back so that she could work with her more. Sarah came often after that, and they quickly became friends to the relief of Brian who was glad to see his young wife so happy. One day while Anna worked on a painting of Sarah, she told her about Robert. Sarah cried as Anna talked about their last day together and asked if she ever felt that she had made the wrong decision by leaving. Anna assured her that despite the pain she felt at the loss of Robert, she knew that she had done the right thing for all of them though it had been very difficult to do.

Lilith often visited Anna and expressed her concern about Anna being alone as her pregnancy became more advanced. Anna told her about Sarah and Brian and that Sarah kept a close eye on her, which made Lilith feel much better. She arrived one day as Anna was working on yet another painting of Sarah and was struck by the bond that had developed between the two women in such a short time. She asked Sarah to sign a release so that she could sell her portraits and offered her a substantial model's fee for each of them, which made her very happy. Brian worked very hard, but he did not earn much money, and this was a real blessing for them.

The days grew shorter and colder, and one morning Anna awoke to find the world wrapped in a shining, white coat of glittering snow. She couldn't wait to get out into this wonderland and grabbed some bread and cheese to nibble on as she made her way carefully down the slope toward the bridge that Brian had built. The sun was warm, but it was too cold for paints, so Anna had brought her sketchpad and worked quickly to catch the early morning light on the snow trying to capture the hushed mystery of the morning. There were little people now living under the bridge, and she sketched them as they scurried around before returning to the house around noon to sit by the fire and warm her hands and feet as she ate lunch.

Once she was well into her sixth month, she stayed closer to the house than she had in the past content just to look out over the scenery and enjoy her retreat. She drove to church every Sunday and often attended classes at the church during the week. Brian had gotten both swings up, and there was also a rocking chair on each porch, so when the days were warm enough, she would sit on one of the porches and sketch. During the evenings she painted the scenes she had sketched during the day, read books that had been recommended by Lilith and Lynette or just sat in deep contemplation letting her mind wander wherever it chose. At these times she often saw the angel and the luminescent being as well as scenes of strange places of unrivaled beauty.

The winter months passed quickly, and as she approached the time of birth and became quite large, she was very careful not to venture out on her own. Lilith began coming out on Saturday and staying overnight so that she could drive Anna to church on Sunday, and Brian and Sarah stopped in every day. She had hired Brian to stack wood on the porch and empty ashes each day so that she didn't have to risk the steps, which gave him a good excuse to check on her.

She awoke early one morning in February with a dull ache across her low back and figured she must have slept wrong. She started breakfast thinking that moving around might help, but the ache persisted as she finished eating and began her daily cleaning. She was leaning over to make the bed when she felt a sharp pain that began in her back and then moved into her lower stomach. She stood leaning on the bed until the pain stopped then finished making the bed. The sun was up by now, and the day was quite warm for this time of year, so Anna gathered her paints and went to sit on the porch in the warmth of the sun. She had no sooner gotten everything on the porch than she had another pain that lasted for a while and then went away.

Anna sat stunned as she suddenly realized that the time had come for her baby to be born. She took everything back in the house, placed a table beside the bed and put cord, scissors, towels, a mirror and a basin of water as well as a glass or water on the table. She had bought several small portable electric heaters primarily for the bathroom and bedroom, and she got these going and filled both wood stoves and banked them a little to make the wood last longer because she knew she would not be able to keep the fires burning in the stoves. She then got a sheet of canvas that she had bought to use when painting the house and put it on the bed with a sheet and some heavy towels on top of it to protect the mattress.

As she worked getting everything ready, she had to stop quite a few times to wait for pains to pass. Her water broke just as she finished, and she hurried to clean that up. She then got on the bed and pulled a light cover over her and looking up saw that her mother, father, the angel, the luminescent being and many elementals were in the room. The pains grew closer and more intense, and she tried to remember what she had read in the books on childbirth. She concentrated on her breathing and used the mirror to check her progress as the small voice seemed to coach her. Just as she finally saw the baby's head begin to crown, she heard a knock on the front door and Sarah called out to her. Anna yelled for her to come in relieved that she would have help and someone to care for the baby. Sarah entered the bedroom and immediately turned to tell Brian to build up the fire and heat some water as she placed a chair beside the bed.

She wiped Anna's brow with cool water and held the mirror so that Anna could see her baby being born. She soon held a beautiful, perfect baby boy up for Anna to see, and they both laughed with relief as he turned bright red and protested loudly at being taken from his warm, comfortable haven and brought into this cold, dry place. Sarah tied and cut the cord as she called for Brian to bring some warm water and cleaned him up before placing him in Anna's arms. She had Brian bring more warm water and then sent him from the room as she tended to Anna. When the afterbirth had been delivered, she gathered all of the soiled linens and the canvas from the bed, sponged Anna and helped her put on a clean gown before leaving to put the linens to soak in cold water. She told Brian he could go on in now as she teased him about having to repair the hole he was wearing in the floor.

When Sarah returned, Anna said she wanted to formally introduce them to Francis William Tindall as she handed him to Brian who acted much like someone with a hot potato quickly kissing him on the head and passing him to Sarah. Saran cuddled and kissed the infant as she crooned a lullaby. She had admitted to Anna that she wanted a child very badly, and Anna saw tears spill from her eyes as she held Francis. Sarah handed the baby back, and Anna felt a lump in her throat as she looked into eyes like those she loved so much. Anna was very tired, and Brian and Sarah went into the other room to let her rest. She guided the little head to her breast and marveled as he greedily took the nipple in his mouth and began to suck, and they soon fell asleep with him nestled in her arms as her mother and father kissed each of them, and the angel wrapped them in her wings.

Sarah stayed with Anna for the next two days while Brian checked on them often as he worked and took care of their place. On Saturday Lilith came as usual to take Anna to church and told them she would stay until Monday when she had to open the gallery. Anna had gotten out of bed the morning following the birth and had fully recovered by Monday evening when Lilith left with the promise from Sarah and Brian that they would watch her closely. They were all amazed at how quickly Anna had adjusted to motherhood and how Francis responded to her voice and touch.

Chapter 22

The weather grew warmer, and as the earth awakened from its sleep, Anna painted feverishly to capture the beauty that was all around her. She had made arrangements for Brian's brother to clear the brush from around the house and the orchard, and he kept an eye on her as she wandered the property with her painting bag over one shoulder and carrying Francis in the basket that she had bought just for this purpose. Francis thrived on all of the fresh air and attention, and his eyes remained the deep blue that everyone had assured her would change. He was always beside her while she worked, and one day she noticed him playing with the gnome as he gurgled and tried to grab him. She felt excited to think that she would finally have someone who could share this magic world with her.

Sarah came by often, and one day as they sat on the porch on a warm summer afternoon, she began to cry as they watched Francis cooing and playing with his toes nearby. Anna felt Sarah's pain as she gathered her in her arms and wished she were able to give her what she so desperately wanted. Suddenly she began to feel a tingle going through her body, down her arms and into her hands. Her palms became very warm as she felt a pulsing energy passing from her hands into Sarah. The two young women stayed like that for a few seconds and then Sarah dried her eyes seemingly unaware that anything had happened and apologized for being so selfish as Brian drove up. She knelt and kissed Francis lightly on the head as she passed him on her way to the truck and waved as they drove away.

After Sarah left and Francis was asleep, Anna picked up a book to read for a while before going to bed. She had bought the book quite a while back and just put it on a shelf. As she began to read, she was struck once again at how what she needed was always given to her. The book explained about the use of energy healing, and Anna was very happy, as she knew without a doubt that Sarah was going to have the baby she so desperately wanted. The church offered various healing classes, and she signed up the following Sunday for a class that was to be held after church for a few weeks. Over the next couple of months, she studied and practiced the healing exercises whenever she had an opportunity.

During the time that she had spent with Sarah, she had become aware that her beliefs were very fundamental, and she resisted the temptation to tell her what had happened. She was very relieved the day that Sarah and Brian came to tell her the good news, and she insisted they let her take them out to dinner to celebrate. They went to a nice restaurant that she and Lilith had gone to once but not to the restaurant where she knew that Lilith and her friends would be.

Their friendship remained strong, and since Sarah did not drive she often joined Anna on shopping trips. Anna noticed that Sarah always stopped to look longingly at fancy clothes and furnishings and talked about how wonderful it would be to live in the city. She often said she couldn't understand why Anna lived in such a tiny little house in the country when she could have the best of everything, so Anna was not surprised when they came one day to tell her that Brian had gotten a job with a good salary, and they were moving to town. Brian came by himself the next day and said Sarah was busy packing for the move. Anna could tell that he was unhappy about this, but when she tried to talk to him, he said he had to do what was best for the family now that they were having a child. Something in Anna wanted to scream out that he would shrivel and die inside if he gave up what he loved, but she knew that everyone has to live their own live and make their own choices. She helped Sarah pack and when the time came arranged to pay for a truck to move them telling Brian that it was free because it belonged to a friend. She hugged them goodbye as they drove away, and then she and Francis returned to their little house.

Anna missed Sarah, but she had more time now for painting, and the demand for her work continued to grow as she used the techniques she was ever improving on. She discovered a tiny clearing where the stream formed a shallow pool surrounded by trees and plants that formed a privacy screen, and this quickly became her favorite place to paint. The orchard did much better now that it was being cared for, and she learned to preserve pears, cherries, plums and apples. The real work on the house was finished, and after Brian left, she asked his brother Patrick to do the few things that still had to be done in addition to caring for the grounds. Patrick was very quiet and kept his distance, but Anna was aware that he kept a watchful eye on her and Francis in case they should need help, which made her feel comfortable and protected. As fall arrived she took shoots from the rose bushes and other plants she had found on the property and planted them close to the house and placed small wooden boxes on their sides under the plants for the elementals to shelter in. She planted climbing roses, jasmine and honeysuckle beside the porches and had Patrick build trellises for these to climb on.

She stopped to visit Sarah a couple of times when in town, but she always seemed to be busy with parties and shopping. The last time that she stopped Brian was there, and she was saddened by the droop of his shoulders and his lack of spirit as they talked about their life here. She saw the longing in his eyes when she talked about the orchard and learning to preserve the fruits, but this bored Sarah, and Anna soon left realizing with sadness that they had taken different roads, and it was time to let them go.

She stopped by to see Lilith, and they talked about the nature of friendship and how people come and go in our lives. They then talked about more personal relationships and how much harder it is to move on when those end. When Anna left that day, she was feeling sad and decided to drive out to where she had lived with the Burkes. As she drove past Robert's farm, she saw that it was deserted. Dread settled over her as she wondered if something had happened to Robert, and she decided to stop and visit with Mr. and Mrs. Connors to find out what had happened.

Mrs. Connors came to the kitchen door when she heard the car drive up and cried out with joy when she recognized Anna. She hurried out and called to Mr. Connors who was working in the barn nearby to come see who was here. Anna went around the car to get Francis, and Mrs. Connors reached for him exclaiming what a handsome boy he was as she ushered Anna into the house. Mrs. Connors offered her a cup of tea and they starting asking questions. Anna was telling them about how she spent her time when the new maid came in and she realized with a start that it was Alice, Robert's older sister. Anna quickly turned away pretending to be taking care of Francis, and Alice didn't recognize her as she left after telling Mrs. Connors that she was going to do the laundry.

Mrs. Connors told Anna that Alice had come to work here shortly after she left because the first maid did not work out. She said Mr. Tindall had died last year and Mrs. Tindall and Jeannie had moved to town and gotten jobs there. Once the rest of the family had left, Robert sold off his equipment and joined his mother and sister in town and was now working in a factory. Anna's heart broke at the thought of him working indoors away from everything he loved. They told her that he had dated some of the local girls after she left but never for any length of time, and Alice had told them he was still single.

Francis began to get fussy, so Anna rose to leave just as Alice came back in. This time she recognized Anna and looked from her to Francis. As Francis looked up and smiled, she saw his eyes and suddenly realized that he was Robert's son and that this was why Anna had left so suddenly. Alice followed Anna as she hurried to the car and asked why she had not told Robert about his son. Anna explained that Robert already had so many burdens, and though she had begged him to let her help he wouldn't, so because she loved him so much she had to leave rather than become one more problem. Anna waved as she drove away worried that she had made a mistake by coming here today, but then she heard the small voice whisper, "Everything is as it should be" and knew that it was meant to be and would work out best for everyone.

Chapter 23

A few weeks after her visit to the Burkes' home, Anna was returning from the orchard one day when she saw Lilith's car stop in front of the house. She began to walk faster to meet her and then stopped suddenly placing the basket with Francis in it and the bucket of apples on the ground beside her, as she saw the man who had gotten out on the passenger side start down the slope toward her. Her heart began to pound as she recognized that familiar walk and saw the beloved face coming ever nearer. When Robert was standing in front of her, he reached out and gently wiped away the tears of joy from Anna's face and took her into his arms with her head cradled in his neck. She clung to him like a drowning person clinging to a life raft, and then raised her head to look into his eyes. He covered her lips gently at first and then with growing passion as all their pent up emotions came boiling to the surface. They continued to hold each other and kiss deeply until Francis began wailing demanding attention. Robert picked up his son and held him high overhead laughing as Francis squealed with delight and Anna felt her heart soar as she stood watching her two men together for the first time.

They turned and started back up the slope with Robert carrying Francis and Anna carrying the basket and the apples. Lilith had stayed by the car, and as they neared the top of the slope, she got in the car waving as she drove away reassured that everything was fine and she was no longer needed. They sat in the swing on the porch, and Robert told her how Alice had finally convinced Mr. Connors to bring her into town when she had some time off to tell him about seeing Anna and the baby. She didn't know how to find Anna, but Mr. Connors had dropped Anna at Lilith's gallery and told Robert where it was. It had taken him quite a while to convince Lilith to tell him where Anna was, but she had finally agreed when he admitted what a fool he had been to let his pride cost him everything he cared about. He talked about how desolate everything was after she left. Then when his father died and everyone else left, he realized that he had sacrificed his chance for happiness for nothing except foolish pride. There was no longer a reason to keep trying to make the farm successful, so he moved into town and took the factory job. Anna talked about how lonely she had been without him and what a comfort his son had been to her even while she carried him. They worked together fixing dinner and cleaning up, and he watched as she fed Francis and put him to bed. Then without a word they walked together to the bedroom and slowly began to undress each other. They made love and then fell asleep in each other's arms reluctant to part even in sleep.

They awoke the next morning to the sound of Francis laughing and cooing, and she got out of bed to go take care of him. When she entered the room, she was not surprised to see that he and the gnome were playing. She built up the fire to take the chill out of the air and had just changed him when Robert came into the living room. After Anna had fed Francis, they sat down to eat and talk about their future.

Anna knew that the time had come when she had to tell Robert about the special world that was so much a part of her life and her spiritual beliefs that were so different from what most people believed. She dreaded this because she knew that all their future happiness depended on his reaction. She cleaned the kitchen while Robert got acquainted with Francis, and then she suggested that they take a walk. She took a blanket for them to sit on and Francis' basket in case he wanted to sleep, and they walked hand in hand with Francis chattering happily in Robert's arms.

When they reached the stream, Anna spread the blanket and sat with Robert's head in her lap while Francis crawled around and played. She told Robert that she had something very important to talk to him about and broached the subject by telling him that she really saw the fairies, gnomes, angels and other things that she painted. At first Robert thought that she was joking, but as he looked into her face he realized that she was serious. He sat up not knowing what to say, and she continued by telling him about the day her mother died, and she found the magical stone cottage.

As she talked, he remembered times that she had seemed to step around something when nothing was there and appeared to be watching something that he could not see. She explained that the elementals were here to care for the earth and that angels were here to help and comfort people. She told him about the gnome coming to help her with her painting and then to comfort her the last day that they were together before she left. She then told him about the day that Francis had been born, and the room had been filled with elementals, the angel, the luminescent being and her father and mother who were all there to watch over her as she gave birth.

As Anna talked about the things she had been told about life and death by her father and the luminescent being, Robert felt a stirring and a joy and peace that he never felt before. They talked all day while she fixed lunch, fed Francis and cleaned the kitchen, and he asked questions while she explained as much as she could. Robert talked about how he had always felt a sense of connecting with something greater than himself when he worked with the earth and how empty he had felt since he left the farm.

She talked about everyone having the ability to heal and do wonderful things and told him about Sarah's baby. She then said that she believed everyone has a purpose for his or her life and even though she didn't know what her purpose was, she would have to be free and willing to go wherever life led her. The more she talked, the more Robert felt himself responding and wishing to be a part of whatever it was that she would be doing.

Because of his attitude about money before, she explained that she was making more money than they could need, but she had to be certain that this would not be a problem for him. He had listened with total attention when she had explained how everything we need is given to us if we only let it happen, and he told her that he was sure he could accept this now. They went to the gallery late that afternoon and then to the restaurant where Robert listened in fascinated confusion as their friends discussed a myriad of subjects and felt growing enthusiasm for the future with these friends and the wonderful woman he loved so much.

The following day Anna drove Robert to the house he shared with his mother and sister to pack his clothes. Mrs. Tindall had been worried when he didn't come home but soon forgot about that when she saw her grandson. They talked as they carried his belongings to the car, and then he handed his mother the keys to his truck. Anna told them how to get to the house and said they were invited to come anytime. They waved goodbye as Robert pointed the car toward home and their new life together.

Chapter 24

On Sunday Anna and Robert made arrangements for a very quiet, simple wedding ceremony to be performed the following week with just a few of their closest friends present. They spent the winter days roaming the land and getting to know each other. She told him about the healing classes she was taking, and he said he would like to learn about healing with plants and foods, so they both began taking classes once or twice a week. Of course she still painted, and it seemed that with her new level of happiness she became even more sensitive to everything around her.

One day as they walked through the orchard, she reached out to touch a tree and suddenly knew that something was wrong with it, so they drove over to Patrick's and asked if he would check on the orchard. Patrick told them that the tree had a fungus that would kill it if it were not treated, and he and Robert talked about what needed to be done. They also talked about the things that Robert wanted to do in the spring with planting a vegetable and herb garden and made plans for Patrick to begin preparing the soil as soon as possible. While they talked, Anna leaned against the tree and felt its gratitude.

After that, whenever Anna walked through the grounds she made a point of touching trees and plants to learn if anything was needed to help them. She also became very excited when she realized that she could study the energy field of any living thing and actually see where there was a problem by a difference in the color or breaks in the aura. She worked with Robert having him sit with his back against a tree and led him through meditation to connect with the spirit of the tree in order to develop his sensitivity to living things and ability to work more closely with them.

Anna had written several times to her Aunt Helen but never mentioned anything about Robert or Francis. She had received no reply and felt sad at the loss of this connection to family and the happiness it could have brought them all. They also visited Robert's mother and Jeannie several times, but were distressed that they only dwelled on how little they had and how poor their lives were. Robert's mother mentioned several times that she would like to live in the country again, and Anna felt guilty about not inviting her to live with them. However, she and Robert agreed that this would never work because she would not be happy with them either, and they refused to let her discontent color their life together. After much urging from Anna, Robert finally agreed to their giving his mother money regularly to help make her life easier, and they made arrangements with the bank to have a check sent monthly.

During the winter months Anna decided she would like to do healing at the church one day each week for a small fee in order to use and develop her skills. Robert always stayed with her and took notes, and when they got back home he researched which foods and herbs would help with the particular problem of each person. By spring they were working as a team with such good success that they were unable to see everyone who came to them in one day, so they talked it over and decided to do healing two days a week. They agreed to limit the time to only two days in order to ensure enough time for Anna's painting and the other things that they were interested in as well as to allow for time with their son.

They often talked about how frustrated they were by people who kept returning with the same problems and never followed any of the advice that Anna and Robert gave them to help themselves. For this reason, and to be more in line with what others were charging for similar services, they decided to increase their fee and donate most of the money to the church. They hoped this would encourage only those who were serious about wanting help; of course they did make exceptions whenever they learned of someone who needed help and really couldn't afford to pay the full price.

As the weather warmed, they were both much busier with Anna painting furiously to catch the breathtaking beauty around her and Robert preparing the soil and planting, but they were never able to stay apart for more than a few hours. Francis ran freely between them, and the gnomes and fairies watched over him, so they never worried that he would come to any harm. One hot summer day when they went to the pool to cool off, Anna did a painting of Robert with Francis lying across his chest both asleep beside the pool in the hidden clearing with the elementals all around them. Robert made a frame for this painting, and she hung it where she could see it often as it represented all that she held dear in her life. When Lilith saw the painting, she asked to be allowed to sell it, and was surprised when for the first time Anna refused to let her have a painting to sell.

They were all very glad when the weather began to cool and things slowed down at last. They sat on the porch each evening after dinner listening to the night as it settled in around them until the chill drove them in to bed. They worked together preserving fruits and vegetables in order to have naturally grown foods, and they sold the excess to friends from the church. Because of the amount of work, they had finally hired Patrick's wife Laura to help with the canning and preserving. Laura was very energetic and bubbly and happy, in contrast to Patrick's quiet steadiness. She was very easy to work with, and they learned a lot from her since she had experience with these things.

The days passed quickly and except for the two days that they did healing and Sundays when they went to church, they seldom left the property. The three of them were very happy with their world and never felt lonely because the more they studied and worked together the more they connected on a deeper level with each other and everything around them. Robert became adept at sensing the earth and growing things though he was still unable to see the things that Anna and Francis saw. Anna and Robert also discovered that by mediating together their lovemaking touched them on a spiritual level and took them to much greater heights of awareness in all areas of their lives. Anna seldom saw her parents now, but she still saw the elementals, the angel and the luminescent being that she had learned was her master guide, and the gnome often sat with her while she painted.

Francis went with them when they did healing, and one day just before he had reached his third birthday he walked over to a woman who was waiting and touched her on her stomach. Robert was about to call him away when he noticed the woman beginning to cry and hurried over calling to Anna who was in the other room with a client. Robert told her what had happened, and when Anna reached the woman's side she saw that there was a tear in the aura where Francis had placed his hand. She told the woman she would see her next and returned to the client she had been working with. She worked quickly to finish with this client and then had the woman come to the private room. When Anna questioned the woman about what had happened, the woman said that she had just been told she had cancer of her ovary on that side.

Anna could usually see a different color in the aura when something like cancer was present, and she was confused because she saw only the tear in the aura. As she worked, with the woman, she found another area where she sensed a possible tumor and had Robert bring Francis into the room. She asked Francis why he had put his hand on the woman, and he said he saw a hurt. Anna then asked if he saw any other hurts, and he pointed to the area where Anna had found the tumor. She told him that he could touch it if he wanted to and watched as the color of the aura cleared leaving only a tear in the aura as Francis placed his hand over the area. When she checked the energy field, there was no longer any evidence of the tumor.

Anna had mixed emotions about Francis' ability to heal being grateful for the gift but also concerned for his safety. She had learned how to protect herself while healing others to keep their problems from transferring to her, but Francis did not know how to do this and because of his age she was unsure how to handle this. That night she and Robert talked and decided they needed to ask for advice on how to protect Francis, so the following day they drove in to see Lilith. Anna had brought more paintings, so they talked about these for a while before broaching the subject of what had happened with Francis and their concerns for him. Lilith agreed that they should be concerned and took them to see an elderly gentleman that Anna had met before who explained how to clear anything that Francis might have picked up. He also suggested that she do this daily since Francis was so sensitive he could pick up things from anywhere without her being aware of it. Before returning home, they took Lilith out to dinner at their favorite restaurant and stayed late visiting with their other friends that they seldom had a chance to spend time with except for a short while after Church on Sunday.

Everything seemed to thrive, and after the crops were in they made arrangements to attend a weekend seminar in a city a short distance away. They were unable to take Francis because of his age, and Anna was concerned about leaving him, but Lilith had said she would keep him and take him each day to the elderly gentleman to have him cleared. Anna had never been away from Francis for more than a few hours since his birth and was concerned what his reaction would be. However, when they told Francis that he was going to stay with Lilith for a few days, he was very happy and excited. They had a wonderful time meeting new people and hearing new ideas and viewpoints on subjects that they were interested in, but they were both happy to collect Francis at Lilith's when the weekend was over and get back home. Anna was reassured about having left Francis as he talked about what a good time he had with all the elementals that lived with Lilith and how much fun they had been to play with. He asked if they could have a swimming pool like Lilith's so that he could swim when it was hot, and they reminded him he had the pool that was very special.

That fall and early winter they concentrated on studying, Anna's painting and healing and just enjoying their life together. Her paintings were in great demand and Lilith had been concerned that Anna would not paint now that she was so happy with her family, but instead it seemed as though she were even more inspired and painted more. Many of the paintings now were very ethereal, and when Lilith talked to her about these, Anna told her these were things she saw in her meditations. Though Anna had never traveled, some of her paintings were obviously of other countries, and Lilith wondered if she were painting scenes from past lives as many of these were of ordinary things that were seldom seen in books.

Francis continued to go with them on the days they did healing, and they kept a close eye on him. Most of the time he was just thrilled to have other children to play with, but he occasionally seemed drawn to someone, and Anna and Robert never interfered except to make sure he was cleared immediately afterward to protect him. They talked openly in front of him about the healing process and the importance of protecting yourself when doing this work and began to show him what to do when he wanted to help someone in order to protect himself.

Anna received a letter from her Aunt Helen early in December and tears of joy filled her eyes as she read. Helen apologized for having been so judgmental and turning her back on Anna when she should have stood by her. She said she had finally told the family about Anna leaving her job because of the pregnancy, and they would all love to see her and her baby whenever she could come. That Friday Anna, Robert and Francis went to visit Helen arriving in the mid-afternoon in order to allow some time before everyone else got home. Helen answered the door and burst into tears as she gathered Anna into her arms and led them all into the kitchen where Anna introduced first Francis and then Robert, her husband. Helen had no doubt that they were father and son, and she wondered why Anna had not told her that she had married her baby's father. As they talked, Helen drew Francis onto her lap, and Anna noticed him touching Helen's chest. She watched as a muddy colored spot in the aura cleared leaving only a slight tear that she knew would heal quickly and said a prayer of gratitude for their having been brought here in time to help her aunt. When Uncle Ted and Stella got home from work, they all went out to dinner, stopping to invite the others on the way, and then they returned to the house where they stayed late getting caught up on all of the news of each other.

Joan, Ruth and Jeff had all married and each had a child of their own. Anna had forgotten how noisy and exuberant this family was and now that there were more of them the den was even worse. Francis, who was accustomed to people who were quiet and sedate, was at first confused by all of the noise as they all talked at once and joked and teased each other, but he enjoyed all of the attention and was soon having a wonderful time playing with the other children and the adults. When it was time to leave, Anna and Robert invited all of them to come for a visit anytime and gave directions on how to reach their home. They all agreed to get together during the holidays and after much hugging said goodnight. As they drove home with Anna snuggled next to Robert, they talked quietly about what a difference love makes in a family, as Francis slept exhausted in the back seat smiling happily in his sleep.

They received a letter from Helen the following week asking them to come for Christmas dinner and drove into town the next day to shop for everyone. They got caught up in the hustle and bustle of the season and returned home tired and happy loaded with gifts, decorations and wrapping materials. Though they enjoyed being with others, they still treasured the quiet times and were grateful to have had their first Christmas together alone. They stopped to drop off presents for Jeannie and Robert's mother on the way to Aunt Helen's and were relieved to get away because the talk seemed as usual to be focused on all that was negative in their lives. Everyone had brought food to Aunt Helen's for the dinner, and once again they had a wonderful time and drove home satiated by the amount of food they had consumed.

Aunt Helen and Uncle Ted became regular visitors to their home and seemed to enjoy getting away from the city, and Anna and Robert often stopped by on the days they were in town for a short visit, so they all grew increasingly close. The cousins occasionally came with their parents, but they all had busy lives and friends of their own, and Anna sensed that Helen was lonely. One day Helen and Anna sat in the sun on the porch on an early, cool spring day while Robert took Ted to look at the orchard. Helen remarked how this place had an almost magical quality and that Anna herself seemed different here. Anna talked about the first time she had come here and immediately sensed something special. They talked about how it always seemed peaceful and somehow apart from the mundane world. Anna always wore the loose, flowing clothing that she loved so much when she was home even when she was painting. Helen asked where she found things like this, and Anna told her about the one regular clothing store that sold this kind of clothing. However, she did not mention that she bought most of her clothes from Lynette.

Anna talked about the healing that she and Robert did, but was very careful what she said and never mentioned what had happened with Aunt Helen's own healing. She was surprised one day when Aunt Helen broached the subject of religion and expressed confusion and doubts about what the church taught. Anna explained the basic principles of what she believed and Helen listened intently as she talked about a loving God who is ready to give us whatever we want if we only live by the principles of faith and love. As they were leaving that day, Anna handed Helen a book that explained the basic principles of metaphysics and told her to read it only if she felt it was right to do so. Anna received a letter the following week thanking her for that book, and the next time they were in town she took other books that she was led to select for Helen.

As Francis spent time with Anna's relatives he became confused because he was teased whenever he talked about the little people he saw. He would be starting to school soon, and Anna and Robert agreed they had to prepare him to be with people who did not believe as they did. They talked to him at length explaining that he had a very special gift that many people would not understand. They also talked to friends from the church who were parents and who faced similar problems, and they established a group of parents and children to meet once a week for discussion to teach the children how to deal with others who believed differently from themselves. Some of the older children came and spoke to the group about their experiences, which was of tremendous help in emphasizing how hurtful people could be. The parents explained the differences between their beliefs and fundamental religions being careful not to be judgmental and stressing that these were merely different, not wrong.

As usual when spring came Anna couldn't wait to get out early and start painting the fresh beauty of the earth as it awoke from its winter sleep. Robert teased her that he had to learn to cook in order to keep them all from starving, and he brought food to her each day as she worked frantically against time to capture the beauty before it faded with summer. Of course he became very busy himself working with Patrick to get the crops planted. Robert had become very knowledgeable about growing foods naturally, and he had a large garden of herbs and roots that he prepared for use in healing as well as for cooking. He also got some chickens so that they could have fresh eggs, and Francis helped him take care of them and gather the eggs. Anna loved to watch her two men working together and often painted them at menial task or when they took a break, and at these times she always said a prayer of thanks for the blessing of these two in her life.

As the weather became hotter, they all spent more time just relaxing and cooling off in the hidden pool. Anna noticed that she was feeling very tired and lazy and assumed it must be the heat, but one morning she awoke with very familiar nausea and knew that Francis was not going to be an only child much longer. That night she told Robert the news and they lay awake a long time talking about the wonder of their life together. The next morning they told Francis about the baby and laughed when he asked if they could go get it now so he would have someone to play with, and they explained that babies take time. This time she could hardly wait to tell Aunt Helen about being pregnant, and wrote a letter the next day to give her the good news.

Chapter 25

Anna and Robert talked about how much working with healing meant to them and how important they considered it to be, but it was becoming more and more difficult to be away for two days each week, and as Anna's pregnancy progressed, they found they had to cut back to only one day a week. As they sat talking on the long summer evenings, an idea began to take shape, and in the fall they talked to Lilith to get her opinion about building a healing center on the front of their property. They envisioned a center where other healers could also work to offer a wide variety of techniques and even classes on various subjects if there was enough interest.

As soon as they started talking, Lilith remembered thinking that this place was going to be very special someday, and she encouraged them to go ahead. They had not been taking any of the money from Anna's painting out of the bank because the land had been supporting them, so there was more than enough to build the center and furnish it with everything that would be needed. Lilith was a shrewd businesswoman and suggested that they see an attorney about legally donating the land and separating the center from themselves to protect them from liability while maintaining control of it. She gave them the name of an attorney she knew and offered to help in any way that she could.

They talked to the attorney and took care of the paperwork before asking Patrick for advice about hiring builders. Each night they drew and revised plans until they finally had one that they felt covered everything they wanted for the center. There had been times that the church had been unable to have events because of limited space, so they started with a very large room that could be divided by sliding partitions. They included another room that was smaller but still large enough for fairly large classes and meetings, a medium sized entryway with room for casual gatherings with an office on one side, six small treatment rooms, four bathrooms and a kitchen area all built in a U shape with a walled courtyard behind the entryway, and all rooms, except the bathrooms, having a view of the courtyard. They met with Patrick and plans were made to start building as soon as all the crops were in and things settled down in the fall.

There was much to do that summer with the usual work and final planning for the center. Anna enjoyed wonderful health with her pregnancy and was busier than every with all her normal duties, her painting and planning and revising all the details for the center. There was great demand for the foods they canned and preserved, and that year they hired an extra girl and an extra man to help with the work. The love between Robert and Anna grew, and they often made love on hot summer evenings outside under the stars after putting Francis to bed, and they discussed erecting a gate to restrict access to private areas of the property if it became necessary to ensure their privacy. As the days grew cooler, and the work slowed down, the time finally came to begin work on the center. Patrick had made arrangements to hire crews for different parts of the job, and he and Robert planned to oversee the work carefully.

The night before the building was to begin, the three of them walked up the trail to the site to enjoy the early evening. Anna suddenly saw her guide, the luminescent being, standing right where the center would be and heard the small voice telling her that this was her purpose, and they were all proud of her. She looked at Robert, who apparently saw nothing, but Francis pointed excitedly, and when Anna looked back she saw that her mother, father and the angel had joined her guide. She explained to Francis that the man and woman were his grandparents as Robert watched them both wishing he were able to share this special gift with them.

Once work began on the center, Anna found herself unable to stay away and had to be careful not to get in the way of the men working. On the weekends Aunt Helen and Uncle Ted as well as people from the church often came out to check the progress. One Saturday afternoon, Helen and Anna were sitting on the porch having a cup of tea while Francis and the men looked over the construction when Lilith drove out for a visit. She joined Helen and Anna, and they sat talking as the sun dropped low on the horizon casting a warm, pink glow over everything. This was the first time that Lilith and Helen had spent more than a few minutes together, and they seemed to really enjoy each other's company. They talked about Anna's painting and Helen was surprised when Lilith told her how successful she was because Anna had always just passed it off as doing well.

With the sun down, it became quite cool, and Anna asked Lilith to stay for dinner, as they went inside to start cooking. They lingered over dinner where the conversation was concerned with the usual general subjects as well as the different things that would be offered at the center while Lilith, Anna and Robert were careful not to discuss subjects that might offend Helen's and Ted's religious beliefs. Because of the long drive, everyone left shortly after dinner was over and the kitchen was cleaned. Francis had fallen asleep and after dressing him for bed and tucking him in for the night, Anna and Robert bundled up and sat outside in meditation looking at the stars for a long while before going to bed.

Work on the center moved swiftly and by Thanksgiving the basic structure, rough plumbing and electrical work was finished, which made it easier to work during inclement weather. Anna and Robert decided to have a large Christmas party in the center on a Friday night even though it would not be finished, and they invited Robert's family, Anna's family and the people from the church. The workers concentrated on getting the large meeting room and the bathrooms and kitchen working, and Anna hired Laura and her sister Doreen to help with the cooking and decorating. The night of the party a light snow had fallen, and the center was decorated and lit with hundreds of tiny lights in many colors. Long makeshift tables had been created by the men and covered with red tablecloths, candles and decorations, chairs had been rented to assure that everyone was comfortable and Christmas music played softly in the background. A large tree stood at one end of the room with many gifts underneath divided into three sections. There was a section for family and close friends as well as sections for generic gifts for women and men for more casual friends.

Since Robert's family had never visited before, he drove in to get his mother and Jeannie, and the rest of the family was to follow and take them back home. They arranged for both families to come early so that they would have time together before the other guests arrived. Robert returned with his family before anyone else arrived, and Anna met them at the door. Anna and Robert had sent Nora a large amount of extra money as a gift so she could afford to buy clothes in an effort to make them feel more comfortable. They filed into the room, and Anna's heart ached for Robert as they talked about nothing but how much everything had cost and how they could have put the money to much better use than throwing it away on a party. Anna had worn one of her more conservative flowing gowns, and they joked about her wearing a nightgown, while Nora made hinting comments about how this would be a nice place to live.

Once Anna's family arrived, things got a little better, but Anna could see that Robert was hurt by the way his family acted, and she made an excuse to get him alone to remind him that he had chosen this family for a reason and that everyone would understand that. He kissed her soundly and remarked that one of the reasons he loved her so much was her wisdom as he bent and kissed a breast and caressed her intimately. Anna pulled away feigning shock, and they returned to the party arm in arm with smiles on their faces. Helen had noticed Robert's obvious discomfort and was glad to see that Anna had managed to make things right for him. She marveled again at this very special person who happened to be her niece and was grateful for a second chance to get to know her better. Anna and Robert handed out gifts to the family before the other guests arrived. He stood with his arm around her shoulder and she squeezed his hand as some members of his family made more remarks about the waste of money but most of them were really pleased, and everyone seemed to relax more.

The food was served soon after the other guests arrived, and when the tables were cleared, the remaining gifts were handed out and everyone began to circulate and Patrick, Laura and Doreen were given their gifts and asked to join the party. As soon as the tables had been cleared, Robert's mother came to tell them goodbye, and they noticed that the rest of the family had already gone outside, and Anna and Robert walked out with his mother to say goodbye and invite them all back any time. The night was a wonderful success and lasted into the early morning hours. Anna and Robert had bought thin mattresses and linens that would be used for the center, and they invited anyone who wanted to stay to do so rather than make the long drive back to town so late at night. The room dividers were put in place to give some privacy, while Helen, Ted and Lilith returned to the house to sleep on cots in the living room and kitchen.

Even though they had been up late, Anna awoke early the following morning and slipped outside to enjoy the peace and mystery of the early morning as the sun rose over the trees causing everything to sparkle. Robert soon joined her, and they sat wrapped in a quilt until the glare of the sun on the snow drove them inside. The others were just getting up, and they all dressed quickly and drove up to the center with food to prepare for breakfast. Everyone pitched in and helped cook and then clean up before driving back to town. Lilith and Anna's family were the last to leave, and they all sat down to have one last cup of coffee or tea together. Helen thanked Lilith for all that she had done to help Anna and invited her to join the family for Christmas at their house. Since Lilith enjoyed being with this family, she happily agreed.

The rest of the holiday season passed quickly and happily with gatherings of family and friends and work on the center. As the weather grew worse and Anna's time of delivery neared, they were happy just to stay home and relax. Francis with the energy of youth spent hours playing in the snow only coming in to warm up occasionally, and Robert often joined him in play, but Anna was content to sit on the porch watching them and saying her usual prayer of gratitude for their happiness. Though she had been very much aware of the child she carried, there had been so much going on that she had not felt as close as she had to Francis, but now she often gently ran her hand over her stomach and talked to the child. Just as she had known that Francis was a boy, she knew that the child she carried now was a girl, and she and Robert had been trying to decide on a name. One day she sat on the porch watching Robert and Francis play, as she ran her hand over her stomach and thought about names. As she thought of the name Diana, the child began to kick vigorously and then stopped as she thought of another name. Since Anna wasn't sure if the kicking was for or against the name, she asked it to kick again if it wanted that name and received one strong kick in response. That night she told Robert what had happened and laughed as the child once again began to kick when she said the name, and they agreed they were probably going to have their hands full with this child if it was this demanding before it was even born.

Anna awoke early one morning in late February with a dull ache in her back and went to sit on the porch wrapped in a quilt to avoid waking the others. She talked to the child as the pains began, and when her water broke, she woke Robert to take Francis and go get Laura to help while she worked between pains to gather everything that would be needed. As she worked she thought about the day Francis had been born and about Sarah and Brian. Patrick seldom mentioned them and when he did it was only to talk about them buying a new house or car or something like that. She thought about how different all of their lives were now and said a prayer of thanksgiving for all of her blessings. When they returned, Laura asked Patrick to watch Francis and tried to keep Robert busy while she gently massaged Anna's back between contractions and supported her during them.

It was late afternoon when the head began to show, and Robert supported Anna while Laura worked to help gently ease the head and shoulders out and then held up their daughter for them to see. Diana did not breathe immediately as Francis had done, but when Laura held her by the feet and gently slapped her fanny she gasped and let out a loud cry. They all laughed nervously with relief as Laura cut the cord and handed her to Robert to clean up as she took care of Anna. When everything had been taken care of and Diana cleaned up, Robert watched as Anna led the little mouth to the nipple for the first time and marveled at the instinct that prompted the infant to start sucking.

Robert went to tell Francis about his new sister and bring him in to meet her. Francis was disappointed when he learned that she was too little to play with yet and asked why they didn't get one that was bigger. While Anna and Diana slept under Laura's watchful eye, Robert and Francis drove to town to tell everyone about the baby. The following day, Lilith picked Helen up, and they came out to help, and Helen said she planned to stay for a couple of days. Anna was still tired and grateful to have help caring for Francis and Diana. Laura would be coming every couple of days to do the laundry and housework, so Anna could just get a much-needed rest. They were careful to include Francis in caring for the baby and Robert spent time alone with him so that he didn't feel neglected. Diana was born on Tuesday and by the weekend Anna was up and except for feeling a little tired and sore was back to normal.

Anna and Helen had a lot of time alone while Robert and Francis were overseeing completion of the center during those days, and they talked about their beliefs. Helen told Anna that she had not been to church for quite a while because she just could not believe what they taught, and Anna asked if she would like to go with them to their church. By this time, Helen had read quite a few of the books Anna had loaned her, and they talked about these at length. Helen still had trouble accepting some of the things she had read, and Anna assured her that she was free to believe as much or as little as she wished. Helen told Anna she had discussed these things with Ted, and he also agreed that the church they had attended no longer met their needs, so they arranged to meet at church the following Sunday.

They sat in silence as they both thought about how much had changed since the day that Anna's mother had died. Anna longed to tell Helen about that day but she sensed that the time was not right yet. That night just as she fell asleep, she felt a light touch on her cheek and looked up to see her mother slowly fade from view. After that Helen and Ted came regularly to church and even took a couple of classes and joined them all at the restaurant after church, and Helen became very good friends with Lilith and Lynette.

With the new baby, Anna was forced to stay closer to the house while everyone else worked to finish the center, so they were often alone. Diana was a very happy baby that responded to attention by cooing and laughing, and Anna found herself holding and talking to her much more than she had Francis. Anna often saw her mother and father standing by Diana's crib and thought how strange this was since they had not done that with Francis, but she thought that maybe this was just because she was such a happy child. She did a painting one afternoon of Diana asleep in her crib with the sun streaming in the window and her mother and father standing beside the crib.

When Diana was just over a month old Anna awoke one morning with a start realizing that she had not cried at all during the night. As she hurried toward the crib in the corner, she saw her mother and father standing in the corner with a little girl. Anna felt as though she could not breathe as she lifted the lifeless little body and held it closely against her. She reminded herself that no life is ever really lost, but that did nothing to ease the pain and emptiness she felt. She sat down in the rocker with the now empty bundle in her arms, and Robert awoke a few minutes later to find her sitting there rocking with tears streaming down her cheeks. They both went outside to sit in the swing huddled together with the little body in Anna's arms and watched the sun rise on a beautiful March day.

As the rays of the sun struck the little face, it reflected into a rainbow, and they looked up to see Anna's mother, father and the little girl smile and slowly fade away. Robert sat in silence for a long time and then told Anna he had finally gotten his wish to see the things she and Francis saw. They talked in hushed tones until Francis awoke and then rose and went inside. They each kissed the little forehead and Anna gently laid the tiny body in the crib. After they had dressed, Robert went to get Patrick and Laura while Anna explained to Francis that his little sister had decided she wanted to go back to heaven. Francis often saw his grandparents, and he knew that nothing is ever really lost, so instead of being upset he just asked if they could get a bigger baby next time that he could play with.

Robert drove to town and told Lilith what had happened, and she contacted the families for them. Helen and Ted came out right away, and Robert's mother told Lilith she had to work but to let them know when and where the funeral would be so that she could attend. That night Anna and Robert were unable to sleep and went outside to sit under the stars. They had been sitting in silence for quite a while when they both felt something and looked up just as the angel folded them in her wings, and they felt relief as they were filled with a peaceful light. The next two days were a blur of people coming and going, and Anna and Robert clung to each other in an effort to ease the pain they felt inside. They buried the little body with a simple service on a knoll beside the orchard overlooking the bridge across the stream, and as they left after the funeral they saw the elementals gathered around the tiny grave keeping watch.

In the days that followed, Anna and Robert often saw her parents and the angel as they returned to their usual routine. The clinic was almost finished, and Anna threw herself into decorating the walls with beautiful paintings of the special world Robert was now able to share with her and Francis. In a secluded corner, she painted the little girl she had seen with her mother the day of Diana's death with a beautiful angel hovering over her. When everyone else had left for the day, she showed this to Robert, and they seemed to get some comfort from knowing that they could always have her there. That night as the three of them walked home in the twilight, they saw Anna's mother and father with the little girl who smiled as they slowly faded from view on the path ahead. They found it difficult to explain to anyone how they were able to accept this loss with such seeming ease, but they felt that this had been a test to move them to an even greater understanding of the true meaning of life and how important it is to make the most of the time we have with each other here.

Chapter 26

By June the building was completed and Anna and Robert made a list of furniture and furnishings they would need in order to open the center, and it was agreed that Anna, Lilith and Helen would take a weekend in the city to make all the purchases. They invited Robert and Ted to join them, but they immediately made excuses why they couldn't go and were obviously relieved when the women agreed to go alone. That weekend Anna picked up Lilith and Helen, and they drove the two hours to the city. Anna had never been here before, but Lilith was very familiar with the city, and they had a wonderful time shopping for the center and for themselves. One day Lilith led them to a gallery that had two of Anna's paintings in the window, and when they went inside she saw there were others. Lilith introduced her to the owner of the gallery who treated her like royalty, which made her feel uncomfortable. Anna had never really thought about what happened to her paintings after she was finished with them and had never considered herself anything special. Helen looked around and realized that she could easily pick out Anna's paintings because they all had a special quality that was lacking in the other works. She saw a painting of Robert and Francis and wished she had one of these. Anna saw her looking at the painting and made a mental note to do one these and one of Diana for her when they returned home.

The trip was very successful, and they made arrangements to have everything delivered the following week. On Sunday morning the three women went to breakfast before starting home and talked about how much they had enjoyed the trip. Anna dropped Helen and Lilith at home and as she drove home she could hardly wait to be back with Robert and Francis in their simple little home. They both ran out as soon as the car stopped, and she scooped Francis up in her arms and kissed him as he squealed with delight. Her eyes met Robert's, and she felt joy spread through her as he took her in his arms and kissed her deeply. She told them about the trip and described the things they had bought and how much they had enjoyed everything. She then told them about the gallery and the way the man had treated her and she felt his attitude toward her somehow tarnished her gift and placed it on a mundane basis.

By the time the furniture was delivered, all of the finishing touches were completed, and a grand opening date was set for the Saturday nearest the summer equinox. Advertisements were taken out in all the local papers and flyers were posted at appropriate businesses. They had healers scheduled for all of the individual rooms that had massage tables in them, and screens had been placed to divide the smaller of the large rooms to provide a place for counselors to work with their clients. They had placed ads to run in magazines beginning the following month and Anna hired Doreen to oversee the daily operation, as she had seemed interested when she helped with the party. She lived within sight of the center and could be available whenever anyone needed access.

Lilith, Robert and Anna had worked together to draw up strict standards for anyone who wished to work at the center in order to ensure that everything done at the center was spiritually based, and anyone who wished to work there would be required to sign an agreement to abide by these requirements. Several people had been turned down already because they were obviously motivated by money rather than a desire to help others. Robert and Anna had agreed from the very beginning that, as in everything else they did, money could not be a deciding factor.

The day of the grand opening was clear and mild with a gentle breeze that kept the many wind chimes hung throughout the building and courtyard chiming merrily. They had hired musicians to play flutes and harps, refreshments were arranged on long tables in the large meeting room and Anna, Lilith and Doreen were set up to book appointments for the healers. When it was time to open the doors at ten that morning the parking lot was filled with cars, people were lined up at the doors, and everyone was busy for the rest of the day. Patrick, Laura and Robert had their hands full keeping the refreshments refilled and directing people for their appointments. Helen and Ted arrived just after noon, and helped give some relief to those who had been working all morning. Lynette arrived around one in the afternoon and offered to work the desk while the others fixed a plate and then returned to the front to eat and help out when needed. Most of the healers were already booked, so things weren't as hectic as they had been earlier in the day. By four in the afternoon only a few clients remained and most of the healers and counselors had left.

As the clients came in they had been given a questionnaire that was coded for the person they were seeing and asked to fill it out before they left to evaluate the service and make any suggestions they had for improvement. When things calmed down, Lynette, Lilith, Laura, Doreen, Helen and Anna began to sort through these and compile a report on each healer or counselor as well as suggestions for improvement. The only problem that they discovered was with one of the counselors who had pushed all of her clients to return to see her every week for at least a month, and Anna and Robert both agreed that she should not be allowed to work at the center. They sent a note to each of those clients to tell them that they should only return for treatment if they felt it was needed and wrote a letter to the counselor notifying her that she would not be able to see clients at the clinic in the future. As the clients left, Anna had questioned them about their results and several times took someone into the office and worked with them herself when they said they felt they had not received what they should have, but overall everyone had been happy with the service and very impressed with the center.

They locked the door at a quarter after four and all those who had worked that day went into the large meeting room to sit down and rest while they talked about the day and made plans for the future. They all agreed that it would probably be good to open the center every Saturday even if it wasn't very busy for a while, and the rest of the time it could be available by appointment only until the demand was great enough to warrant scheduled hours. Robert and Anna had talked about buying a small bus to transport people between the church and the center since they did not want to drive in and do healing there. The few readers who remained joined the discussions when their clients left, and two of them said they would work at the center regularly if they had a bus to transport their clients because they preferred not to work at home. They knew both of these people and were happy to know they would be part of their work, so Robert and Patrick planned to go look for a bus on Monday. Everyone pitched in to clean up, and by six they had all left except Lilith, Helen, Ted, Patrick, Laura, Doreen, Anna, Robert and Francis who was asleep in the office.

They talked for a while longer and then said goodnight at the door, and Anna and Robert walked home in the gathering dusk with Francis skipping ahead playing with the elementals along the way. Lilith had offered to drive them, but they both said they needed some fresh air after the day, and they walked in silence just enjoying the peace after all the noise and confusion. Once they reached the house, they sat on the porch and talked about the day and the things that needed to be worked out for the clinic. As they talked Anna looked to where Francis was playing and a tear ran down her cheek as she saw him talking to Diana and her parents. Robert turned to see what she was looking at and put his arm around her shoulder and pulled her close thankful that he was able to see this himself. They watched as the three faded from view and Francis came to sit on the porch with them and told them that Diana said she really liked the center, but she liked the house better. They were all tired and went to bed early and were lulled to sleep by the sound of the night creatures and the wind chimes as they were stirred by a gentle breeze.

The following day at church they got very good feedback about the center even from people who had not been there and several asked about working there on a regular basis after they learned about the bus. They had a meeting after church to find out when people were interested in working and to schedule for Saturdays. When they got home, Anna and Robert made a list of work that would be needed to keep the center clean and in good shape and to take care of the grounds. They estimated that they needed at least two men to work outside and two women to clean and help can and preserve food as they needed to expand the growing and preparation of food to meet the demand. Since they lived so far out, finding help could be difficult, and the idea of providing small cabins and meals in the main building of the center was discussed. They still had some money in the bank, but they had to be prepared to cover the expenses of the center until it could stand on its own, so this would have to wait for a while.

While Robert, Francis and Patrick went to buy a bus on Monday, Anna worked on a painting of Robert and Francis and one of Diana with her grandparents and the angel over the crib that she wanted to give to Helen. After the noise and chaos of the last few weeks she enjoyed this time alone to reconnect with her inner being. She went to sit by the pool to paint and sat for a while just absorbing the beauty and peace of nature before starting to paint. As she worked on the painting of Diana, she felt a small hand on her shoulder and had to brush tears from her eyes before she could continue. The day passed quickly, but she managed to get both paintings done by the time the light began to fade. When she realized how late it was, she quickly gathered everything and started toward the house where lights were shining in the windows. Robert met her at the door and helped her put everything away as she apologized for being so late. He said he and Francis had gone to look for her but she had been so engrossed in her painting that they didn't want to disturb her.

Francis was bubbling over with the excitement of the day and telling her about the big bus they bought and Patrick let him ride home in it. Patrick had taken the bus home with him until they found a driver because they didn't want to leave it at the center with no one there. He and Robert had talked about the people they would need to work for them, and Patrick said he knew some people who might need a job and would be good workers. That night Anna and Robert talked about how much Patrick and Laura had helped with everything and agreed to offer them a small interest in the center in addition to their salaries.

The following morning they lounged in bed talking and enjoying the luxury of a day with nothing pressing to do until Francis came in complaining that he was hungry. After dressing and eating breakfast they took pencil and paper and sat on the porch making notes of the things that needed to be taken care of. They planned to resume their healing the next week two days each week, and they signed one of the treatment rooms out to themselves for every Tuesday and Thursday for the next three months. They were working on a list of things to discuss with Patrick when they saw him driving up the trail to the house. They could see that someone was with him and assumed it was Laura, but as the car stopped Anna recognized the man getting out of the car and ran down the stairs to throw her arms around him. Robert felt a twinge of jealousy that quickly disappeared when Patrick told him this was his brother Brian. Anna had talked about Brian and Sarah, how they had been there to help when Francis was born and how much she missed them. Anna led Brian to the porch and introduced him to Robert who warmly shook his hand and thanked him for all that he had done for his wife and son. Brian told them that he and Sarah had finally decided to get a divorce because they just didn't want the same things, and he was staying with Patrick while he looked for a job.

Robert told Brian that they needed someone to help take care of the center and the grounds and Brian would be perfect because of his skills. The all walked up to the center to show it to Brian, and Anna saw the way his eyes drank in the every detail of the land as though he couldn't get enough. Brian told them that he would love to work here, and when they reached the clinic he starting pointing out little things that needed to be done or improved on. Brian mentioned that he had to find a place to stay and Patrick told him he could stay with him and Laura until he found a place, so they agree he could start the next day. As they walked back to the house, Anna mentioned the idea that she and Robert had of building small cabins to provide a place for people who worked here to stay since they were so far from town, and Brian assured them that he and Patrick could build these for a lot less than if they hired someone. He told them he would work on some sketches and prices, and as he talked Anna saw his eyes come alive with happiness and enthusiasm for the first time since the day he and Sarah had moved to town.

Chapter 27

By the time the center had been open for a month, all of the little problems had been ironed out and things were running smoothly. Anna was glad to finally have more time to devote to her painting, as this had been neglected while they were so busy. They were into the hottest part of the summer now, and the three of them enjoyed visits to the pool to cool off and relax during the heat of the day. Francis stayed at the center most days even when Anna and Robert weren't there because there were always other children to play with, and Anna welcomed this chance for him to be exposed to other children since he would be starting school in a few weeks.

Brian always took time to talk to Francis and kept an eye on him, and Anna knew that he missed his own son. She had spoken privately with Brian shortly after he first returned and had asked about Sarah and their child. As he talked to her about his son Sean, the sadness returned to his eyes and she could see how much he missed him. He told her that once they had moved to town he and Sarah had grown farther and farther apart, and she had found someone else who wanted the things she did. She had agreed he could see Sean whenever he wanted, and Anna encouraged him to bring Sean with him anytime because there would always be someone to help take care of him.

By the end of summer, the center was paying its own expenses, including those for the bus, and they had a total of three men working in addition to Brian, Patrick and Robert to take care of the grounds and the crops with Anna, Laura, Doreen and one other woman doing cleaning and taking care of the center. Because the center had a larger kitchen than the house, all of the preserving and canning was done there, and it became routine for everyone to meet there after the clients were gone for the day and eat dinner together. The meals consisted mostly of fresh fruits and vegetables that were grown on the property, in addition to eggs, cheese and meat for those who wanted them. Employees were never charged for what they ate, but when those who were at the center doing healing or teaching classes joined them, they were asked to make a donation to cover the cost. While everyone ate, they discussed problems that had arisen during the day as well as ideas for changes, and many decisions were made and problems solved by the end of the meal. These gatherings were very informal with everyone encouraged to join in, so by the end of the summer they were working well together as a team. Although Anna and Robert had the final say in all decisions, they always paid attention to what everyone said, and were careful to explain if for some reason they disagreed.

The center was very busy on Saturdays, and Lilith and Anna's family often came out on Friday and stayed in the center overnight to help out the next day. One Friday when Helen and Ted had come out by themselves, Anna gave them the painting she had done of Robert and Francis like the one that Helen had admired and one of Diana in her crib with her grandparents and the angel standing watch over her. She and Robert told them about seeing Diana with Anna's parents, and Helen wistfully said she missed her sister and wished she could see her. They talked for a long time that night about life and the thin veil that separates us from those who have passed over.

On Saturday, Lilith brought an art dealer, who she introduced as Mr. Stanford, to meet Anna and Robert because he wanted to invite them to a showing of her work in his gallery. As they talked, Anna noticed that he had a rather large area in his aura that looked like something serious in his upper abdomen. She made it a rule to never solicit clients, but she was unable to push this away and finally asked if he had been having any digestive problems. He admitted that he had been having a lot of stomach upset but had not taken time to see his doctor, and Anna urged him to do this as soon as he returned home. She was relieved when she felt the familiar release of tension that she had come to recognize signaled appropriate action to an inner urging.

Anna had been approached many times to promote her painting and had always declined, but Robert urged her to attend the show because he felt it would be good for her to see firsthand how others perceived her paintings. She finally agreed, and Mr. Stanford told them he would make arrangements for hotels and send them directions. The trip would take two days each way, and when they talked to Francis about it he begged to stay home. Brian said he would be glad to stay at the house with Francis while they were gone, and they agreed this would probably be best as he would be bored if he went with them. The following week as they began to pack Anna found that she was actually starting to look forward to the trip. She was excited at finally being able to see the ocean, and when Robert protested as she packed all of her painting supplies, she assured him this was an opportunity she just could not miss. The showing was on Friday and Saturday, so they left Tuesday in order to allow extra time in the event there were problems on the way. Mr. Stanford had made hotel reservations for them along the way and sent a map with details, so they could just relax and enjoy the trip.

They arrived in the late afternoon on Wednesday and decided to take that night for themselves and contact Mr. Stanford the following day. The hotel where they were staying was on the ocean, and Anna immediately unpacked her painting supplies and they headed for the beach. A summer storm was threatening with dark clouds gathering overhead, and she worked quickly to catch the power and intensity of the waves as they crashed onto the shore and the menacing look of the clouds. As she looked out across the water, she saw a sailing ship from a bygone era being tossed wildly by the waves and was barely able to get it sketched in before it faded from view. Robert sat contentedly beside her watching her work and enjoying the smell of the ocean and the salty spray that settled on everything. He seldom had a chance to just sit and watch Anna, and he felt pride well up in his chest as he watched the skill with which she worked and thought about the quiet, gentle strength that was so much a part of her. She had barely finished the painting when they had to grab everything and run for the hotel as large drops of rain began to pelt them and lightening flashed simultaneously with deep rolling thunder. After showering to remove the salt spray, they sat in the dark and let the violence of the thunderstorm wash over them as everything was first lit with blinding brilliance by the lightening and then plunged into darkness. They listened to the waves crashing against the shore before rushing back out and felt the rhythm of the ocean and the power of the storm deep within their being as they fell asleep.

Everything was bathed in the magical glow of a full moon when they awoke a few hours later and dressed to go in search of food, as they were both very hungry. The dining room was still open but almost deserted since most of the guests had eaten earlier, and they talked quietly as they enjoyed a wonderful meal of fresh seafood. After dinner they decided to go for a walk along the beach to enjoy the ocean and the freshness after the storm. They took off their shoes and walked barefoot letting the damp, cool sand and ground shells squeeze up between their toes as the waves washed over their feet and lower legs. They talked about the wonder of their life together and expressed regret for those who struggle so hard trying to get things only to discover that once they have them they only want something else. Robert talked about his family and how much he wished he could have the relationship with them that Anna had with her family. This led to a discussion about the methods they had studied for making the changes you want to make in your life to get the things you want, and they talked about the different things he could try in an attempt to change his relationship with his family. However, they also acknowledged this was probably something he had chosen as a lesson and as such would not be subject to very much change. They returned to the hotel to sleep deeply with the smell of the sea and the salt spray on their bodies as the waves lulled them with the ocean's rhythmic song.

The following morning they went down for breakfast and found that there was a message from Mr. Stanford to let them know he would meet them in the hotel at noon for lunch to make arrangements for the following day. After breakfast they walked through the town and the quaint little shops that sold brightly colored clothing with tropical birds painted on them and knick-knacks decorated with seashells. They purchased several blouses and a few simple souvenirs for their family and friends and a telescope for Francis, before returning to the lobby to await the arrival of Mr. Stanford. The three of them chatted as they ate lunch on the terrace overlooking the ocean, and then Mr. Stanford said a car would be sent for Anna and Robert the following morning at 9 a.m. He invited them to join him for dinner, but Anna told him she was eager to do some more painting while she was here. That afternoon they walked through the town stopping occasionally for Anna to do a quick sketch before returning to the hotel to take a nap during the heat of the day. They took a bath and then lay on the bed listening to the ocean and the seagulls as they drifted off to sleep in each other's arms.

Robert awoke to find Anna sitting at the window painting the scene with a large ship far off on the horizon and seagulls flying overhead. She had just slipped on a long blouse over her naked body, and he remained lying on the bed for a long time quietly admiring the unique naturalness that gave her a beauty much more meaningful than the shallow beauty so admired by most. He rose and went to stand behind her while she leaned back against him and continued to paint. At times like this they seemed not to need words and just allowed themselves to become lost in their love for each other. They dressed and took her painting materials down to the beach, so that she could catch the colors and special quality of twilight, which was Anna's favorite time of day. They left everything on the beach and walked barefoot at the edge of the surf until the light was right and then she worked quickly to capture the magic of this time of day with the pinkish-orange glow and the shadows that lent an air of intrigue and mystery to everything. Anna painted until the moon was high overhead while Robert walked the beach in search of special shells and small pieces of driftwood, being careful to stay close in case Anna needed him, and then returned to lie quietly beside her lost in meditation.

The following morning they had breakfast in the hotel dining room and entered the lobby to be told that the car had just arrived to take them to the gallery. Anna had only been to Lilith's gallery and one other, and suddenly felt hesitant when the car stopped in front of a large building in the heart of the city. The gallery had not opened yet, and Mr. Stanford met them as they walked toward the door and led them into a large building with vaulted ceilings. On the right about midway of the building Anna saw that dozens of her paintings were hung in a small alcove with access to adjoining areas through archways. She had never seen her paintings displayed professionally before and was surprised by the effect that proper lighting had. The paintings had more depth, and it seemed as though the characters had come to life. As she moved around the room, she realized that Mr. Stanford had been collecting her paintings for a long time, as many of them had been painted during the days when she had still worked as a maid. As she moved along the walls, she could see the changes in her life reflected in the paintings and became aware of her own growth emotionally and spiritually. Robert could see the profound effect this was having on her, and he and Mr. Stanford moved away to leave her alone.

As she reached the archway that marked the last of her paintings, she looked into the adjoining area and was taken by surprise by the paintings there. They were all hard, bold lines and strong colors in direct contrast to her soft lines and soothing colors. These paintings were of the physical world in bare, raw honesty of beauty and ugliness mingling, which made Anna feel slightly uncomfortable, and she wondered why Mr. Stanford had put these side by side with hers. She moved to the archway between the two areas and stood looking from one to the other and suddenly realized the genius of this placement. It emphasized perfectly the contrast of the two sides of humanity itself caught between the stark reality of the physical world and the soft, mysterious, illusive world of spirit. She turned excitedly to talk to Robert about this and almost ran into another woman who was also looking from one room to the other. As their eyes met, they both smiled as they realized they were looking at the other artist. Anna was wearing one of the flowing dresses of swirled pastels that she loved so much, and the other woman was wearing a very tailored suit of black and white. Anna held out her hand and introduced herself to the woman who in turn introduced herself as Ada, and they stood talking about painting in general terms until Robert approached and Anna said goodbye.

They moved around the gallery stopping as a painting caught their eye until they noticed people beginning to come in and returned to the area where Anna's paintings were hung. As they listened to the comments of the people who passed through the gallery, Anna was surprised to find that many people totally rejected her paintings as silly and fanciful while being completely captured by Ada's paintings. She had never thought much about this, and she found herself seeing things from a different perspective as she listened to the different comments.

Lunch had been catered for the artists in a room upstairs and Anna enjoyed talking to the different artists as they ate. She made the observation to Robert that the room seemed to be divided with her at one end and Ada at the other with the remaining artists scattered between according to where they felt most comfortable and some in the middle who seemed comfortable with both. There was a ceremony after lunch to introduce the different artists, and following that they were asked to return to their respective areas to answer questions. Anna knew that Robert was getting bored and suggested he go for a walk or something for a while as she returned to her alcove. She answered many questions about her subjects and was very careful how she answered except when talking to several people who made it clear they believed as she did in the other realms. There were several paintings of Robert and Francis, and she glowed with pride as she talked about her husband and son.

The afternoon passed quickly, but Anna suddenly realized that she was very tired. Looking up, she saw Robert approaching with a cup of tea, and he told her that the car was there to take them back to the hotel. As they moved toward the door, Mr. Stanford approached to say goodbye and Anna had a chance to discuss his placement of her paintings next to Ada's. As they talked, she noticed once again the same problem in his aura, but she hesitated to mention it here. Mr. Stanford told them that the car would take them wherever they wanted to go tonight and would pick them up again the next morning. Anna and Robert agreed that they only wanted to go back to the hotel and maybe take a walk after dinner after the busy day, and they sat in silence as the car moved through the city streets. Anna had never really like cities, but some of the architecture was truly beautiful, and she realized that the city at night had a certain beauty with the windows lit as though inviting one with a hint of secrets to be told. Unlike the day when people moved hurriedly along not noticing anyone else, at night couples walked slowly hand in hand and smiled as they passed others.

Upon reaching the hotel, they went to the dining room for dinner and then to their room to change before going to sit on the beach. Anna was too tired from the day to paint, and they sat talking about the things they had observed and the insights they had gained that day. Robert told her how proud he had felt to be there with her and that he realized even more how fortunate they were. He had overheard two women talking about how wonderful it would be if the world were really like her paintings, and he had longed to tell them that it is if you only let yourself believe and be open to it. He had suddenly realized he had lived in the physical world of harsh reality until meeting her and they now shared this magic world. They walked slowly along the beach letting the water wash over their feet and legs before returning to their room to sleep curled up together. It rained during the night, and the soft patter of the rain mixed with the crashing of the waves, and Anna dreamt of a land beneath the sea in which mermaids and sea creatures lived.

Many people visited the gallery the next day, and Anna was glad when the day was over even though she had enjoyed meeting some of the people and had exchanged addresses with some and invitations to visit. They planned to leave the next morning and thanked Mr. Stanford for everything as they said goodbye. He thanked them for coming and told them that he had sold almost all of her paintings for a very good profit, in part because some people had been so impressed by her, and that this more than covered any expenses. As they said goodbye, Anna felt compelled to ask Mr. Stanford if he had seen his doctor yet and was told that he had an appointment for the following week.

Chapter 28

They both awoke early the next morning eager to be on their way home to their friends and family and decided to eat breakfast on the road as they were getting tired of the hotel food anyway. The trip home was uneventful, and they stopped whenever they wanted taking their time and enjoying the drive. The closer they got to home the more eager they felt, and they did not stop at all the last two hours. As they turned on the road that led to their property, they unconsciously leaned forward trying to catch a glimpse of the center. It was dinnertime, and everyone was still at the center, so they stopped there rather than going on to the house. Everyone was talking and had not heard them enter, and they stood for a moment looking in silent thankfulness at these people who made up their world before moving into the room to be greeted by laughter, kisses and hugs. They sat talking late that night while Anna and Robert told everyone about their trip and got caught up on all the news. Francis sat between Anna and Robert and seemed reluctant to leave their sides, and Brian said he had really missed them.

After putting Francis to bed, Anna and Robert sat on the porch for a while letting the peaceful beauty and mystery of the place seep into their being. They looked up to see Anna's mother and father and Diana smile and then slowly fade away as though they had also come to welcome them home. They were glad to be back in the comfort of their own bed and slept late the following morning until Francis bounded on the bed demanding breakfast. He and Robert wrestled on the bed while Anna threw on a wrapper and went to build a fire to take off the chill and cooked. When breakfast was over, they went to sit on the porch in the warm morning sun while Francis ran and played in the yard with the puppy that Brian had gotten while they were gone to take his mind off missing them. Anna had at first resented Brian doing this without their consent, but when she saw how happy Francis was she and Robert both agreed it was something they should have done themselves.

Anna had realized on the trip that she was going to have another child but had wanted to wait until they were home to tell Robert. That morning sitting in the swing she took Robert's hand and moved it to her stomach as she told him the news, and he gently wrapped his arms around her smiling broadly. They told Francis the news when he came to sit on the steps and rest for a while, but he didn't seem too interested now that he had his dog and plenty of playmates at the center and would be starting school in a couple of weeks.

The weather grew cooler, things slowed down after the busy summer, and everyone had more time on their hands; and one Saturday night the talk over dinner turned to the need to build cabins for single employees and for visitors. Several of the healing rooms in the center had been used for this, but the center was becoming so busy that these rooms were frequently needed. That day they had really needed the room Brian was staying in. Patrick and Brian had been keeping the books for the farm and the center respectively with Robert keeping an eye on everything, and there was more than enough profit to buy supplies to build two cabins. Brian had drawn several plans for the cabins since he returned, and they all discussed these and chose a larger one for employees, since it would be a home for them, and a smaller one with just two bedrooms and a small common area for guests who would only be staying for a short while. They decided to begin work on a cabin for Brian immediately, and the three men went to order building supplies on Monday morning.

The first day that Anna and Robert took Francis to school was very hard for her. They had talked the night before about his gift and the problems it might cause, but he said he knew from playing with the other children at the center that he could not say anything about the things he saw because they would laugh at him. Anna was relieved when he came home very excited and eager to return the next day.

After Francis went to bed, Anna and Robert talked again about how everything in life impacts everything else and how diffcrent their lives might have bcen if they had made different decisions. Robert pointed out that if Anna had quit her job as a maid once she began to make money from painting they would never had met, and if she had kept her job but spent the money on frivolous things, she would have been unable to leave when she became pregnant. They speculated about how different their lives would have been if she had married him and lived with his family in that atmosphere and the effect it would have had on their love for each other. They both said a prayer of gratitude that Anna had been strong enough to make the decision she had for all of them.

With Francis at school each day and the men working on the cabins, Anna was alone more than she had been since first moving here. She enjoyed good health and was up early each morning and was out with her painting as soon as it was warm enough to begin. She went often to the private pool, and one day as she sat quietly painting a picture of the undersea life she had dreamt about while on their trip the gnome came and sat beside her. She was very happy to see him as it had been a long time, and they talked about the turns her life had taken in the interim. She had never painted his picture before, and that day she asked it he would mind, and he gave his permission. She set aside the painting she had been working on and began to paint the gnome while they talked until the shadows grew long and she had to return to the house to clean up for dinner.

The following day Anna headed once again for the pool but suddenly found herself on the path to the magical stone cottage. She recognized it immediately and walked quickly to the door and knocked. Once again the other gnome opened the door and then disappeared as soon as she stepped inside. She walked to the table where the book lay open to the day she had last been there and sat down to read. As she read, half forgotten memories were brought to the surface, and she began to see the pattern that had been woven by the decisions she had made since the last time she was here. Of course, when she reached the present day, the rest of the book was blank, and she felt excitement when she wondered what wonderful opportunities lay ahead. She looked to the other side of the room where she had seen her father before and was not surprised to see that her mother and Diana were there with him. They talked to her about the mysteries of life and told her they were very proud of her before fading away. She sat for a while just enjoying the wonder of this place before walking out the door and up the path to find herself back in familiar territory and turning to find that the cottage had disappeared. She continued to the pool where she finished the painting she had started the day before. That night as they sat looking at the stars before going to bed she told Robert what had happened and the things that her parents and Diana had told her about the mysteries of life and the universe.

Brian was able to move into his cabin in two weeks and while he worked to finish it Patrick and the other men started the second cabin. Anna and Robert were still doing healing two days each week and more when a real need arose. The busses made several trips back and forth to town three days during the week and all day on Saturdays. They had many very good healers who worked regularly at the center now, and people came from ever increasing distances as the center's reputation spread. The cabins had cost less than expected, and the decision was made to build a couple with just one bedroom and a bathroom for those clients from out of town who needed an inexpensive place to stay while getting treatments. Within two months, four cabins were finished and in use practically all the time, and Robert and Anna decided to build a cabin closer to the house for friends and family to use since their place was going to be very crowded after the new baby arrived, and they decided at the same time a room should be added for Francis now that he was getting older. By Thanksgiving all the cabins had been built and Francis had his room, so Lilith and Anna's family came to stay over the Holiday. They had a wonderful Thanksgiving dinner in the center with family, friends and all the employees except Doreen who still took care of the front desk at the center and helped with food preparation.

Anna had sensed that Doreen might have a problem but neither she nor Laura said anything, and Anna did not want to pry. However, the Saturday after Thanksgiving when Doreen came to work she was obviously upset and Anna decided it was time to push the point. She had one of the others take over at the desk and led Doreen into the office where Doreen broke down in tears and said that her husband had started drinking very heavily and was now threatening her. Anna offered to let Doreen have one of the cabins and assured her that she would be safe with all the men around to keep an eye on her. This had apparently been going on ever since Doreen started working at the center but had gotten to the point that Doreen was afraid to go home. At the end of the day, Patrick, Brian and Robert took Doreen to get her things and made it very clear to her husband that he was unwelcome anywhere near the center.

Doreen was soon back to her normal happy self and life settled into a quieter routine as Christmas approached and winter settled on the land. Anna often painted sitting in the sunlight on the porch now. With Francis away all day at school she and Robert were like young lovers free for the first time to make love whenever they wanted. They both laughed as Anna remarked that after all these years of marriage they were finally having a honeymoon. On nice days they would find a secluded spot on the property where Anna could paint, and they often made love surrounded by nature the way they had when they first met. They had made it very clear to everyone that their privacy was not to be intruded on, and those who worked there made certain this was respected.

Chapter 29

Anna had written to tell Robert's family about the new baby, but they had not seen them for quite a while, so the week before Christmas they went by his mother's house to invite them for Christmas dinner. Nora made excuses that they all had to work, and as they left Anna and Robert admitted that they were relieved. To ease their feelings of guilt, they returned a few days later with expensive gifts for everyone as well as money and food for them to have a really nice dinner. Christmas that year was a wonderful affair with the center decorated and full of people celebrating the glory of the season. Lilith and Anna's family stayed from Christmas Eve to after New Years, and all of her cousins came out on Christmas Eve. They all pitched in to prepare the large dinner for Christmas and cots were set up all over the center to accommodate anyone who wanted to stay overnight.

After the festivities were over and everyone ready to settle down for the night Anna, Robert, Francis, Lilith, Helen and Ted walked back to the house slowly in the clean, crisp air under a full moon. Anna walked between Helen and Lilith and said a prayer of gratitude for these wonderful women who shared her life and the blessings they brought to her. It snowed during the night, and they all walked back to the center for breakfast throwing snowballs and playing along the way. After breakfast was over and the center had been cleaned and returned to order, most of the guests left to drive back to town while the employees, Lilith, Helen, Ted, Anna, Robert and Francis talked and made plans for the coming year. They decided to build a few more cabins and add a wing onto the center with treatment rooms and medium sized classrooms, as there was more than one class almost every night of the week and some during the day. There was plenty of food left, and they ate a late lunch of leftovers before going their separate ways in the late afternoon taking food to snack on later.

The center was quieter than usual between Christmas and New Years and everyone enjoyed the chance to rest. When Francis started back to school and Lilith, Helen and Ted returned to town the men worked when the weather permitted on the new wing of the clinic, so Anna once again had time to herself. After she reached her seventh month, she contented herself with painting in the house and preparing for the baby. She knew the child was a girl and she and Robert talked about a name finally deciding on Roberta Anne.

Anna's paintings had a wide range of subjects now, and Lilith said they were selling as soon as she got them in. Most of her ideas came in dreams and were often of strange worlds that she had never heard of and places that she had never seen. She and Robert had talked about traveling once the baby was old enough and she looked forward to visiting the places she saw in her dreams including mountains and deserts.

The winter days passed quickly and on a cold crisp day in April Anna felt the low ache begin in her back and sent Robert to get Aunt Helen and Lilith. She was not afraid, but both she and Robert found it impossible not to remember Diana and had agreed she should have as much help as possible. Robert stopped at the center to have Doreen and Laura go stay with her while he was gone and asked Brian to pick Francis up at school and keep him out of the house. Anna's contractions were very close together by the time that Helen and Lilith arrived, and Laura was very relieved to see them, as she had always felt a little guilty and wondered if she had done something wrong when Diana was born. Roberta was born just over an hour later with no complications and immediately made her displeasure at the whole process known much to everyone's relief. Francis was brought in and seemed quite unimpressed but said he guessed it would be nice to have a little sister. He seemed so grown up now and Anna missed her little boy.

Helen and Lilith stayed for the next week to take care of Anna and the baby and help in the center while Laura and Doreen did the cooking and cleaning. Brian and Doreen came to the house together one evening to visit Anna and the baby, and Anna was happy to see that they were becoming more than friends. She brought up the subject of a divorce for Doreen and offered financial help if it was needed.

Anna felt fine within a week, so Lilith and Helen returned home. The first day after they left Robert stayed close to the house until Anna finally told him to go find something to do because he so obviously wanted to be out helping with the early spring preparations. That afternoon she was very tired but assumed she had just done too much too soon and vowed to take it easier the next day. During the night she awoke burning with

fever and shaking with chills and Robert sent Francis to bring Doreen and
send Brian for Laura while either he or Patrick went for Helen, Lilith and
a doctor. When the doctor arrived he told them that this was an infection
that sometimes happened after childbirth and could be very serious. He
gave them some medicine and then left saying he would check back the
next day. The medicine seemed to help with the fever and chills and they
all felt relieved. That evening Robert saw Anna's father, mother and Diana
standing by the bed and looked at Anna to find her smiling as he heard
Diana say that it was time for mommy to come with them because her job
was done. Robert gently kissed Anna and whispered that he would always
love her, and she answered that she would always love him and be with
him as she took one last deep breath and passed gently away. He watched
in agony as she left the body on the bed and went to join the others who
were waiting for her while pain seemed to be trying to tear his chest from
his body. The others were unaware that she was gone until Lilith noticed
the tears coursing down Robert's cheeks and moved to the bed where the
empty shell that had been Anna lay.

Epilogue

Anna and Diana often appeared to Francis and Robert and one late evening when Robert and Helen sat on the porch in the twilight they looked up and both saw Anna and Diana with Anna's mother and father. Helen cried copious tears of joy as she saw her sister once again young and healthy in the company of her loved ones. As they slowly faded away, Anna's mother thanked Helen for taking good care of Anna.

Helen had stayed for weeks to help take care of the children and comfort Robert, and she and Ted finally decided, with Robert's blessing, to sell their house and move here since Ted had been thinking about retiring. In time Lilith also sold her house and gallery and came to live close to those who were her family after Lynette had passed.

Shortly after Anna's passing, Mr. Stanford had written to thank her for insisting that he go to the doctor because he had been found to have cancer that had it been left unchecked would have caused his death. Though he had been sick for quite a while, he was now well and very grateful. He invited them to visit anytime at his expense, and Robert answered the letter congratulating him on his recovery and informing him of Anna's passing.

Doreen and Brian married after her divorce, and his cottage was enlarged over time as they stayed to raise a family. The close network of people remained intact with the center as their focus and Francis and Roberta grew up healthy and happy surrounded by many who loved and cared for them. Roberta did not have the gift of healing or sight that her father and brother had, and though she loved them both she often considered them strange. She loved music and at an early age asked for first a flute and then a harp, which she learned to play beautifully without ever taking lessons and composed her own music of unequaled beauty and depth. Francis went to college and became a renowned medical doctor, confounding everyone with his ability to diagnose and treat illnesses through the use of medical science, his gift and his father's knowledge of plants and herbs though he never divulged that he used anything other than medical science except to a select few.

Robert never found anyone to take Anna's place, but she kept her promise and was always there whenever he needed her, and many nights he was comforted by her presence beside him while he slept. He often walked alone and one day he looked up to see the stone cottage that Anna had painted shortly before her death. He walked up the path and knocked on the door, which was opened by a gnome who invited him in and promptly disappeared. On a table in the center of the room was a book labeled "Robert's Life" and Robert sat down to read. Many memories returned as he read the story of his life and alternately laughed and cried as long forgotten emotions surfaced once more. The book pointed out important decisions that had changed the course of his life, and he saw how he had grown from a bitter, lonely person into a happy, fulfilled person mostly because of the remarkable woman he had loved so dearly. He wiped tears from his eyes and looked up to see Anna and Diana standing across the room. He stayed a long time as they discussed the truth about life and death and the beauty that lies beyond the veil. He wanted so much to join them, but Anna reminded him that their children needed him and the time would come when they would be together again. She told him of many lifetimes they had shared that had led to this lifetime of happiness. Robert left the stone cottage that day happy and resolved to move forward and live his life to the fullest.